Fiamma

Dana Neri

For my family.
For Rachele.
For girls like Fiamma.

FIAMMA

Fiamma.

Her name is Fiamma, and she loves to play with fire. A fitting name: she is all flame. Like a moth drawn to light. Drawn to it – fatally drawn to it.

As a child, she would watch those strange insects squirming and beating their wings against the scorching glass of a lightbulb. She'd wonder why – though clearly in pain – they stayed there, pressed against the heat, wings pounding the burning surface.

Why didn't they just fly away?

They didn't want to. It almost seemed they were trying to break through the glass, reaching for the fiery core of the light itself. Tiny, mad Icaruses flying toward certain death, burning their wings in the sun. Fiamma always thought moths were foolish – and yet fascinating. Just like her, drawn to intense heat and brightness.

She often remembers the time she was four, when her parents took her to visit an old aunt in the countryside. A massive fire blazed in the middle of the room, in a stone fireplace as old as the house – filled with years, layered with memory. It was the first time she'd seen such a big fire up close. This bold red and yellow mass – strong, unbroken, alive – was far more majestic than the flames that came from her father's mouth during his shows.

That fire was something monumental, or at least, that's how it seemed to her when she was so little. The heat and light it gave off drew her in like a magnet.

Fiamma remembers wondering what that incredible fire could smell like.

As a child, she believed that all beautiful things had a unique smell. Like caramel squares, cotton candy, or her stuffed bear, *Bobo*. Every time her mother put him in the washing machine, she would cry uncontrollably because she knew Bobo wouldn't smell the same for a long time. He would smell like detergent and fabric softener. She preferred him when he simply smelled like himself.

That day at her aunt's house, Fiamma wanted to know exactly what the fire smelled like. She didn't want just the scent of burning wood or ash. She wanted to smell the fire itself, that magnificent mass of reds, yellows, and oranges. So, she crept closer to the fireplace, slowly, step by step, never taking her eyes off the glowing mass.

She realized she was too close when she heard her father shout her name:

FIAMMA!

A moment later, his arms grabbed her firmly, pulling her away from the source of that fascinating light, from its colors and its smell.

Years have passed since that day. Fiamma's father is no longer with her. A stomach cancer took him, carrying him away with stronger, firmer arms than his own. But Fiamma's attraction to fire remains. And now, she is free to burn herself as much as she wants, with no one there to stop her.

I live near a church where every month there are only a few weddings and a lot of funerals. The tolling of the bells accompanies me each day in this house, marking my time, pulsing in my ears, and sometimes, penetrating my soul.

At noon, an endless orgy of chimes. A union of iron and bronze, an obsessive and invasive percussion. An explosion of metallic clangs that drills into my temples.

I've always found the shape of the bells grotesque: the iron clapper swaying in its hollow, brushing the air, slapping the void before crashing against the bronze surface.

Ding.

That same clapper making its way back, slapping the air, brushing the void.

Dong.

And then meeting nothingness cloaked in gravity and vibrations.

Dan.

The sound they make is even more grotesque. The only ones I can tolerate are the funeral bells. One toll, then a pause, then another toll. A rhythm of silence and sound, measured, steady, discreet. Perhaps that's why I prefer funerals to weddings. I enjoy the dignified, measured progression of pauses and sounds. A balanced, dignified sob that cuts through the air without overwhelming it with clangs.

I can hardly remember anything about your funeral.

Sometimes, I find myself watching the funerals of total strangers from my window, trying to find something that will remind me of the day when bells, like those of this stupid church, rang for you. I stare at the faces of the strangers dressed in black, hoping to see something that will take me back to that day. I try to scrape from the crust of their grief a piece of the pain I'm sure I felt too, years ago. But it always turns out to be completely pointless.

I lost you, and I can't even remember when it happened exactly. I know you're gone because your absence is even louder than these clanging bells. It screams louder than all their noise, louder than that vicious clamor that fills my ears. Because your absence surrounds me like an icy embrace, tightening around me in a grip of shivers and emptiness. And it leaves me like this, dazed and waiting, begging for a scrap of memory.

Her father, Daniel, chose the name Fiamma for her. He picked it not only because he was a fire-eater with a deep passion for fire, but also because, when she was born, Fiamma had a full head of red hair that immediately captured the attention of everyone in the hospital. Over time, that hair, which had been straight at first, began to curl, and everyone who saw it couldn't resist running their fingers through her copper curls.

She inherited her hair color from her mother, and in fact, that's the only thing Fiamma feels they truly have in common. She and her mother are either too different, or perhaps too alike, but they never really understood each other, not in the way she understood her father.

Her father was a different story. She always felt a closer connection to him, even though she only had a few years with him before he passed. After his death, when people talked about him, they mostly said he was a good man. But Fiamma never paid much attention to that, it's just what people always say about the dead. What really mattered to her was hearing that he was a rebel, an anti-conformist, a free spirit. Everyone agreed that there was nothing her father could have done other than be a street performer, because he could never have spent his life behind a desk or confined by a schedule. She felt the same way. Restless, always needing to move, always discontent. When people asked what she wanted to do when she grew up, she could never answer. Truthfully, she never even bothered to think about it. She has no idea what she will do, and deep down, she doesn't really care. The one thing she's sure of is that she will never work in an office or live a life of endless work until she's too old and broken to enjoy anything, like waiting for retirement and a meager pension. At that point, she'd rather just die.

Sometimes, she thinks it wouldn't be so bad to become a street performer like her father, but then she remembers that she doesn't have his charisma, his talent, or any special abilities, really. Except for one: she's great at hurting herself. If there were a contest for self-injury, she'd be a finalist, and if she could make a living off it, she'd never have to worry about going hungry.

She's not yet nineteen, but sometimes, she feels a hundred years old. Sometimes, she feels closer to death than to life, and when she's in the waiting room at the doctor's office, she envies those old, complaining people, full of aches and pains but still somehow clinging to life. She watches them hold on to the world with their bony, wrinkled fingers, stubbornly refusing to let go. Their relentless grip fills her with a mix of disgust and admiration. When she hears them speak in their whining, sing-song voices about friends who have passed, she can sense their fear and bitterness, but it's their doggedness she feels most strongly. They won't let go of their place in the world, because that place belongs to them, and no one else. When they tell her, "You're so young, you can't possibly understand… All the pain…" she wants to scream that they're the ones who don't understand. They don't know what it's like to be her age, to spend nearly every day chased by the desire to die. She wants to tell them how it feels to spend her days trying to make sense of it all, digging holes in the nothingness, hoping to find even a single reason to keep going. She wants to spit in their faces, telling them it makes no sense to fight Death while holding contempt for life. She wants to shout to the heavens that, while they envy her youth, she envies their stubborn attachment to whatever's left of who they were and who they still are.

But in the end, she stays silent. Even when she hears them complain about *young people today*, casting sideways glances at her, she just waits for her turn in the doctor's office and silences the voice inside her, the one that's already rotting.

The cancer had ravaged your hands. The magical hands I had seen skillfully handle fireballs and burning embers were now reduced to lifeless sticks, the flesh gone, leaving what looked like a flimsy veil of skin, draped carelessly over your bones. Your hands had lost all their magic. And you had stopped being the indestructible, invulnerable, invincible hero I had always believed you to be.

Thinking back on it now makes me sick to my stomach, because in my childish, selfish way, I must have shown you my disappointment. You must have seen the unease on my face every time they forced me to come to your bedside. You must have noticed how hard it was for me to kiss you when they made me lean in close, how I'd instinctively pull back, purse my lips, and hold my breath. I was trying to shield myself from the taste and smell of something I didn't recognize, to keep the scent of death away.

I wasn't as good as Mom. She was a great actress even then, able to put on the best of smiles the moment she stepped into your room, only to break down in tears as soon as she was safely out of your sight.

She and Grandma were masters at masking their pain. They were so good at it that at one point, I thought they were losing their minds. They could even joke with me about the bags attached to you, or, more precisely, the bags that were attached to your life. The feeding bag and the urine bag. One for input, one for output, and you in between, like an organic funnel.

The day you died, Mom and Grandma stopped pretending. I still clearly remember Mom's scream when she got the call from the hospital. A cry of anguish that pierced the silence that had settled over our house those final days. I remember running to hide in the tool shed in the garden to escape the unbearable sound of her wailing. Outside, the wind was so strong it felt like it was tearing at my head. I stayed there, lost in time, letting my thoughts bleed.

What followed, after her father's death, is mostly a blur for Fiamma. The memories of those days are like old, faded Polaroid photos, unfocused and indistinct. They're scattered and fragmented, with darkness swallowing up the colors and shapes.

In the white part of one of those Polaroids, beneath the hazy image, are her thoughts:

Ten thousand cigarettes – the measure of pain.

In the dark rectangle, Fiamma sees her mother, Sara, smoking her first cigarette. She had always been so health-conscious, so focused on maintaining her body and her appearance. She sees her sitting at the living room window at night, drawing shapes on the dark glass with her cigarette.

The next Polaroid shows an ashtray left in a corner, overflowing with cigarette butts. The ones smoked down to the filter, twisted and shriveled like dried mushrooms. In the white space below, Fiamma reads:

Only ashes remain.

In another Polaroid, Fiamma can make out her grandmother, telling her nursery rhymes. The white area of the photo holds the words to one rhyme they especially loved. They would often sing it, each time with a new tune made up on the spot:

Where there's rain, there'll be a rainbow,
where there's dark, a glow will grow,
and how wonderful to look up high
as colored dreams like balloons fly by.

By, by, byyyyy! Fiamma loved to shout that last word, and her grandmother would laugh with delight.

Her grandmother passed away after about a hundred rhymes, a handful of fairy tales, and a few more years. Luckily, there is no Polaroid to capture this memory in Fiamma's mind.

*

After her grandmother's death, Fiamma and her mother moved into Giorgio's house, the theater producer who had secured Sara a job in his company a few months after Daniel's passing.

Giorgio's house was as grand and ostentatious as his surname, Bernantineschi. Beautiful for Sara, but far too vast for Fiamma. Two hundred and fifty square meters for just three people, which meant more than eighty-three square meters each. In that space, loneliness would often echo endlessly, like a bouncing rubber ball, against the minimalist walls and furniture.

Giorgio was fond of throwing large parties at his home, and Fiamma suspected he invited so many people to convince himself that all that extra space was actually necessary. She couldn't find another reason for the regular festivities that had no particular occasion. Every time she found herself observing the crowd, those colorful dots moving across the enormous white walls, Fiamma felt even more alone. And she knew that clattering noise would never leave her, forever imprinted in her memory.

The DJ would shout, "I wanna see you enjoyyyyy!" and everyone would yell together, overcome by some kind of mystic trance or uncontrollable madness: "Yessssss!"

Some would swing their heads left and right, mouths agape and noses wrinkled, as if imitating pigs; others would punch the air in front of them like boxers in an imaginary ring; and still others would sway their hips, creating awkward, exaggerated ellipses that came off as grotesque and vulgar, not sensual at all.

There were always at least a few couples dancing close, even during group dances. And there was always, without fail, what Fiamma had come to call *the desperation train*: the vast majority of guests would link up in a long, multicolored snake, weaving across the living room in a completely uncoordinated manner. Under the psychedelic lights, Fiamma could only see fragments of bodies, pieces of faces, distorted expressions twisted into forced laughs, forming a single mask. A splotch of color spreading like paint, producing a deafening noise that filled a void even louder and more unbearable.

Fiamma's mother participated in these absurd celebrations, though with little enthusiasm. She would often sit in a corner, sipping her prosecco slowly, smiling ostentatiously but remaining perfectly still when someone invited her to join the madness. Giorgio, however, was the wildest of them all. Usually so composed, serious, and in control, he would become completely unhinged after drinking a bit too much and realizing he was the center of attention. Fiamma knew this Dr. Jekyll and Mr. Hyde side of him all too well. One night, after going to the bathroom while the party raged on, Fiamma returned to her bed to find a young woman there. Her face was streaked with mascara and tears.

"Please...please...let me sleep here with you," the girl mumbled, almost pleading with her eyes as she curled up with her knees drawn to her chest. She reminded Fiamma of an insect, curling into a ball to take up as little space as possible, pretending to be dead when in danger.

"Let me stay...please…" the girl pleaded again, like a trembling insect.

Fiamma was taken aback, unsure of how to respond. After a brief moment of hesitation, she moved to the opposite side of the bed, staring at the girl's profile lit from behind. Her chest rose and fell rapidly, irregularly, almost in sync with the music leaking through the walls and under the door. Black tears streamed from the girl's eyes, but no sound came from her lips.

That night, Fiamma fell asleep feeling even sadder than usual, though she couldn't pinpoint why.

The next morning, the girl had vanished without a trace. It was as if she had evaporated into thin air, leaving only mascara stains on the pillowcase.

I can barely remember your funeral. But I remember so many things about your presence. The smell of pine after you'd showered. The way you'd wander around the house wrapped in that funny towel. The mint-scented aftershave that left a cool, fresh breeze on my cheek every time you kissed me. The times you'd lift me up and spin me in the air, like I was as light as a kite. How your unshaven beard would tickle my face when you hugged me after one of your exhausting nights performing in the square.

I remember all of your shows. Or at least all the ones I was allowed to watch.

People came from far and wide to see you perform because they said you were one of the best. But I always thought you were the best of all.

I'd watch you, entranced, standing at the center of that imaginary circle, surrounded by the crowd, like in a giant game of ring-a-ring-o'roses. You looked even taller, stronger, and more handsome in your brown tunic, your face glowing in the amber light.

You'd blow hard, forming an 'O' with your mouth, and I remember I'd often catch myself mimicking you, forming the same shape with my lips as I watched. It was an automatic, unconscious gesture that showed how much I admired you and wanted to copy you.

The huge tongue of flame that came from your mouth captured everyone's attention, wrapping them in its spirals before vanishing into thin air. It'd tease them for a moment, and then, just like magic, it would appear again.

I remember all my birthday parties. Along with the many gifts you gave me, you'd always perform a special show just for me and my friends. Even the smallest garden would transform into a grand stage that barely contained my pride and the amazement of the other children. Thanks to you, I had the best birthday parties a little girl could dream of. And a collection of joyful memories where I was the star, like a princess in a fairy tale. Thanks to you, I was never afraid of the dragons in stories, papa. And all the children I met treated me with great respect.

Fiamma is in her final year of high school, and this year, or rather, in just a few months, she will face her final exams.

Sometimes, she thinks she should be worried, that she should feel compelled to study harder, but then she finds herself spending entire days staring blankly at her textbooks, with no desire whatsoever to flip through them. She remains lost in thought, absentmindedly playing with her red curls, as though none of it concerns her. Her grades are far from stellar, and she has a school performance that is far from impressive, which will undoubtedly hurt her in one way or another when the time for exams comes. Last year, she was nearly held back due to excessive absences and a violent argument with her Math teacher.

During class, she often ends up staring into space, or at the dirty white walls that are almost grey now. On sunny days, she can sit for hours watching the sunlight filtering through the large classroom windows, transforming into beams of dust particles floating and dancing in the air. She often finds herself wishing she could be as light as those tiny specks of light, drifting along with them, floating above everything. Suspended on top of it all.

She rarely pays attention during lessons, and the voice of whichever teacher is speaking usually reaches her ears as a muffled sound, distant from where her mind really is. The only class she listens to with any amount of attention is Latin, not because she particularly enjoys it, but out of respect for her teacher, Mrs. Belardi. Despite her role as a teacher, which could make her potentially unbearable, Mrs. Belardi is truly a good person. One of those people who is kind to the core, someone who despite life's unfairness has never stopped being positive toward others. At school, gossip runs rampant among both students and teachers, and everyone knows that Mrs. Belardi lives alone, abandoned by her husband after years of infidelity, left to live off her meager teacher's salary and a life without children.

Fiamma's classmates often make fun of her, cracking ridiculous jokes and playing tasteless pranks on her. Fiamma, however, tries to follow the lessons attentively. She watches Mrs. Belardi pacing back and forth in front of the class, impatient and quick, like a soon-to-be father anxiously pacing the hospital corridor waiting for his first child to be born. She feels a sense of tenderness for her teacher, hidden from the world behind thick glasses and dark, heavy stockings. Mrs. Belardi's hands are never still, always moving nervously. Sometimes, they play with a tiny piece of chalk, sometimes with a pencil, or sometimes she draws imaginary circles in the air.

From time to time, Fiamma nods and smiles at her, knowing it pleases her and gives her the illusion that she isn't speaking just to herself or the classroom walls.

"Burgagni, can you recite the most famous verses from Catullus' poem number 5, and tell me to whom it was dedicated?"

Mrs. Belardi looks at her expectantly through her enormous tortoiseshell glasses, behind which her small, tired yet kind eyes peek. She always has a hopeful expression when she asks questions, as if wishing one of her students will finally surprise her with an encyclopedic answer that could earn them a good grade and, perhaps, give her life some meaning.

Fiamma doesn't want to disappoint her, even though she hasn't studied much. She relies on her decent memory and tries to recall what was discussed in class a few days earlier.

"Well, Catullus 5 was written for his beloved, *Lesbia...*" she begins, her voice unsure, as it always is when she's asked a question she's not certain she can answer.

"Very good, Burgagni..." Mrs. Belardi's eyes light up. She's genuinely pleased when a student is prepared, and perhaps especially so when the student is Fiamma, since there is almost always mutual fondness between them.

"And do you remember the most famous line? Recite it in Latin, of course..."

"U-um, yes... *Da mi,*" Fiamma's voice falters, even though she tries to hide it. "*Da mi... bacia mille...*"

"*Basia,* not *bacia,* Burgagni..." Mrs. Belardi corrects her gently, almost regretfully, with the soft tone one might use when correcting a child.

"Ah, yes, *da mi basia mille, deinde centum...*"

"Excuse me, Miss, just a quick question..."

From the back row, Francesco Ramazzini raises both his hand and his voice, making sure everyone notices him. He's one of the classmates Fiamma can't stand, though he's popular at school. A rather unremarkable kid who wears the same football jersey almost every day, one from an English team he can barely pronounce, and who, a few months ago, started the trend of wearing bandages on his face. He always wears at least two near his eyebrows, sometimes even one on his chin, showing them off like medals of valor. These are tiny bandages that mean nothing and serve no real purpose, other than to cover imaginary wounds.

The moment Fiamma sees his smug smile, she knows he's about to make another one of his idiotic remarks. She feels embarrassed for him and sorry for Mrs. Belardi, who has to endure his brainless comments at least twice a week.

"This guy... this Catullus... Why did he keep chasing after this girl if she was a lesbian?"

The whole class erupts in raucous laughter. Ramazzini, having finally made his 'joke of the day' – the one that will make him feel like a big shot for the rest of the lesson – looks around smugly. Fiamma rolls her eyes to avoid seeing his grin or the fake, amused expressions of the others. Every single one of them is laughing, except for her, but she knows that only a fraction of the class actually finds him funny. They're laughing out of habit, not genuine amusement.

Fiamma realized Francesco was an idiot the first time she saw him walk into the classroom with his arrogant swagger, and she gets more confirmation of it every time he mocks the teacher, imitating a sheep and calling her "Baaaalardi."

Mrs. Belardi shakes her head with a weary expression and adjusts her glasses on her nose. Fiamma feels sorry for her but doesn't have the courage to stand up for her in front of the entire class. She doesn't feel strong enough.

"Very funny, Ramazzini, very funny," Mrs. Belardi remarks with ironic acquiescence. "Maybe after I finish questioning Burgagni, you can come up and delight us with your humor, along with your infinite culture."

I know it's dumb to be thinking about death at my age, papa, especially when I'm not even twenty yet. But at my age, a single year can feel like a hundred. Then another thousand. Then a hundred again. It's just like that Catullus poem, the one Mrs. Belardi had us go over the other day in Latin class. A thousand kisses, then another hundred, then a thousand more, another hundred, then a thousand, and again another hundred. "A thousand years, then a hundred more, then another thousand, and then another hundred, then a thousand, then another hundred." I was changing the verses in my mind while the teacher read them aloud. Papa, you have no idea how much a day can feel like a year for me. It's hard to explain, even to myself. But when I see adults, and I see what they can do, how they live, how they 'feel', or don't feel, day in and day out, it just seems like there are so many empty spaces, so much time lost in nothingness, too much useless silence, or even worse, pointless noise to fill that silence. It makes their days seem pointless to me. And I can't help but think that I don't want to grow up. I'd prefer to die now, at my age, now that I 'feel' everything, now that every emotion, good or bad, fills me to the brim. Now that every single day is worth living, never the same as the last. It's so much better to live like this, to feel everything, than to become like most people around me, who've stopped feeling life and don't even notice.

Every day after school, Fiamma meets her best friend, Elife, waiting for her, probably the only true friend she has. They first met a year ago and have been practically inseparable ever since. Elife can't stand most of her classmates either. They see her as a nerdy outcast, obsessed with math and a little clueless about fashion. The truth is, Elife doesn't dress badly, she just doesn't follow the trends most girls her age do. She dresses in a neutral, androgynous way. Most days, she wears black men's dress pants, slim fit with cuffs and creases, paired with a loose white shirt and a black leather vest. Fiamma used to think her friend didn't bother with hygiene because she wore the same outfit every day. But when she visited Elife's house one day, she discovered Elife's closet was full of nearly identical clothes, at least seven white shirts and five pairs of the same black pants. Despite her outfits, Elife doesn't come off as masculine. Her delicate, harmonious features balance out the lack of femininity in her clothing. The truth is, Elife doesn't fit into any specific gender category, and that's probably why her classmates tend to ignore her.

Together, Fiamma and Elife are an unusual pair. One wears anonymous clothes, the other loves eccentric ones. And, of course, neither feels comfortable with kids their own age. As a steampunk enthusiast, Fiamma enjoys wearing brocade corsets with buckles, pocket watches, skirts with studded belts, and belt bags, clothes that mix Victorian style with futuristic elements. The first time she walked into class as a freshman, she left everyone speechless. As usual, she arrived late, just as the bell rang, moments before the teacher. She noticed the stares as she walked to her seat, some surprised, some entertained, and others outright disgusted. She took the only empty seat, didn't greet anyone, and kept to herself. That day, Fiamma made a promise: she wouldn't let anyone mock her for how she dressed, and she would steer clear of anyone who didn't accept her for who she was.

*

"Hey, Fiamma! How was today? Everything alright?" Elife asks, her usual mix of seriousness and playfulness evident in her tone. She says the same thing every day, in the same order, with the same voice. Elife's life is full of small rituals, repeated phrases and routines that stay pretty consistent. Sometimes it's tough for Fiamma to keep up, but Elife is by far the most real and fun person Fiamma's ever had around.

"Yeah, it was fine," Fiamma responds. "Mrs. Belardi quizzed me on Catullus. She said I did well overall, just slipped up on a couple of verses and some declensions. Still a solid grade. She's so nice though. I love her as a teacher. If all teachers were like her, school would definitely be more fun. How about you?"

"Great! I had a math test today, and I think I totally nailed it!" Elife responds, practically jumping with excitement. Her sky-blue eyes sparkle behind her thick, blue-rimmed glasses. Fiamma's always thought Elife was cute, but she's convinced her friend would look stunning without those giant glasses. They cover too much of her face, making her eyes seem tiny and weighing down her nose. But Elife never takes them off, almost as if they're part of her superhero persona, hiding the secret to her powers.

"I have no doubt you crushed it. You're a math genius! I don't know how you enjoy it, those science subjects just bore me to tears!" Fiamma teases.

"You're totally wrong!" Elife fires back. "My amazing grandpa, Anacleto Passolunghi, a math enthusiast and a bit of a philosopher, always said Math is fascinating, beautiful, and the ultimate truth."

Elife says it with such conviction that Fiamma bursts out laughing. She knows Anacleto, even though they've never met, since Elife quotes him all the time. Fiamma can't keep track of all the proverbs and sayings Elife has shared with her, her quirky, adorable best friend probably has a whole section in her brain dedicated to them. Elife, or just Eli. Sometimes Fiamma wonders what she'd do without her. Sometimes she wonders how she even managed before meeting her.

"Yeah, yeah, maybe you and your genius grandpa are onto something," Fiamma smiles. "But as your super friend Fiamma Burgagni, I'll tell you: Math is a major pain in the ...!"

*

Eli walks Fiamma home every day after school. Her bus stop is just down the street from Fiamma's house, and it comes by every fifteen minutes. So, the girls linger in front of Fiamma's building, chatting until the last possible moment. They walk hand in hand, like a couple in love.

Fiamma's hands are always cold, even in hot weather, while Eli's are always warm and a little sweaty, even when it's chilly. They stroll slowly, talking about the little and not-so-exciting things that happened during their school day, and making plans for after homework or over the weekend.

"I can't meet today because I have to take my brother's girlfriend's little brother to a party at four," Eli grumbles, trying to keep up with Fiamma, who's walking at her usual brisk pace. "I just don't get why I always end up doing this. Probably because I can't say no! I mean, my brother's girlfriend's little brother, seriously? I don't even know him. I don't even remember his name, honestly. Or maybe my brother didn't even bother telling me. I don't get it. Why does this have to fall on me? Why don't his parents take him, or his sister, or my brother, for that matter? What's it got to do with me and my brother's girlfriend's family?"

Fiamma can't hold back a laugh, even though she knows she shouldn't, out of respect for her friend.

"Oh, come on, Eli… maybe you'll end up having fun at the party. And anyway, I think people ask you to do things for them because they know you're nice and always say yes."

"Yeah, yeah, but I'm honestly getting tired of it. And how could I possibly have fun? It's a party for little kids! Anyway, I'm busy today. But tomorrow I'm free. It's a special day for someone special!" Eli winks at Fiamma in her usual silly way, squinting one eye too tight and pulling a funny face. "So, have you decided what you want to do for your birthday, which also happens to be the first Sunday of spring?"

"Need you ask? Shopping, obviously!" Fiamma grins widely, knowing full well that Eli can't stand shopping.

"Or, more like window shopping, which is what I'll be doing. I'll just stand there drooling in front of the store windows, imagining I can buy things with my hopes and dreams. I'm broke, so yeah, buying anything's not happening!"

"Shopping… *obviously*…" Eli responds with a tone that's anything but excited. "Fine… since it's your birthday, I'll sacrifice myself to the altar of consumerism! I'll drag my unwilling body from one store window to the next!"

"I just don't get how you can't love shopping, Eli. Seriously! If it were up to me, I'd do nothing but shop!"

"Well, if it were up to me, I'd probably spend all my time in front of a computer or reading comics… we all have our things! Anyway, see you tomorrow afternoon?"

"How about four o'clock? I'm supposed to meet my mom for lunch, though, if she actually shows up. She's already canceled on me twice. They say third time's the charm, right?"

"She wouldn't cancel on your birthday! Alright, four o'clock it is. I'll meet you outside, and please, at least for once… try to be on time!"

Eli says the last part while pointing her right index finger at Fiamma, as if giving her a warning. She knows her friend is always, hopelessly late.

Fiamma smiles and promises to be on time, even though deep down, she knows she won't be able to keep that promise. She's just one of those people who can't help but be late.

When Fiamma sees Eli's bus coming, she quickly says goodbye and almost pushes her friend away, worried she might miss it. She watches as the bus drives off, disappearing around the corner. As she unlocks the door to her building, she feels a wave of loneliness. She thinks about how Eli is like the sister she never had. Since meeting her, Fiamma has learned what true friendship is and what it really means to care deeply for someone. When she imagines life without Eli, she feels a tightness in her chest and stomach, like she's struggling to breathe, and it makes her feel nauseous.

I really wish you could have met Elife, Dad. She's my best friend. Probably the only real friend I've ever had. She can't stand her name, though, since it was given to her by her parents in honor of her great-grandmother. But I actually like it; I think it fits her perfectly. Elife. Like e-life, electronic life… kind of like how e-mail stands for electronic mail. Mrs. Belardi would probably say 'nomen omen', you know? You'd like my Latin teacher, Dad. She looks like the typical older teacher: glasses that always slide down her nose and clothes that smell faintly like mothballs, but she's tough as nails. She's the only teacher I have who really loves her job, who chose to do it because she enjoys it, not just for the paycheck. I think you'd like Elife too. She's definitely a bit quirky. But you never really liked 'normal' people, right? You always thought they were boring, and I'm a lot like you in that way.

Eli spends most of her time on the computer. She's a total tech geek and knows all kinds of crazy programs that I can't even pronounce. She's almost painfully routine, and has this obsession with numbers, stats, and percentages. A couple of months ago, she actually stopped talking for a while. She told me she'd come to the conclusion that only a tiny percentage of the things we say every day are worth saying. I'm not even kidding! One day, I got a text from her saying she'd done some statistical analysis on what people say, and she found that only about 30% of what we say actually has meaning or purpose. She said the rest are just words we say out of habit, politeness, or just to fill space, clichés, trivial stuff, empty chatter. I remember reading that and thinking, "Oh, great, I'm going to be stuck with a semi-mute robot, having to do all the talking". But eventually, she agreed to loosen up and talk more, even if it meant saying some pointless stuff every now and then.

Eli doesn't have many friends, and she's never had a boyfriend, even though I think she's really pretty. She's got these beautiful sky-blue eyes and a huge mass of curly black hair. Tomorrow afternoon, we're going shopping downtown. Well, actually, I'll be window shopping, dreaming about all the things I'll never buy, and Eli will come along, pretending not to be bored to death. But hey, that's what friends do, right?

Sometimes, when Eli and I are out together, I catch myself thinking about how great it would be to come home and tell you all about my day, about all the fun we have, the smart things she says (she's always so clever), the goofy things I say, and the dreams we talk about.

Yeah, I really wish I could share all of that with you. Oh, and I almost forgot: one more thing Eli and I have in common, we've both lost our dads. And from what I understand, she was just as close to hers as I was to you.

I know it might sound bad, but when I'm with her, I feel a little less like a loser and a little less alone. It's like there's someone who really understands what I'm going through.

Today marks the first day of spring. Today is her birthday. Another birthday without her father. The first one spent in a home different from the one she shared with her mother. She calls it her *one-tomb apartment*, this tiny place she moved into as soon as she turned eighteen. She was born on March 21st, just like Alda Merini, the poet she admires so much. Yes, today is the first day of spring, and it's a beautiful, sunny Sunday, but Fiamma doesn't feel like there's much to celebrate. Even the wisteria that hangs in heavy clusters from the roof of the house across the street seems dull and scentless. Its frail violet fingers and wilted lavender blooms struggle to push through the slightly misaligned tiles, trying to carve out their space in the emptiness, but without much success. It almost seems to mock her, this futile, aimless climb, as she watches from her window. It's almost as if it's whispering to her that everything in life is pointless, even pain – especially her pain.

Fiamma stares at the wisteria and accepts the challenge. She's determined to prove that it doesn't always have to be that way, that pain doesn't have to be meaningless. Sometimes, it can become something more beautiful, something that transforms and gains a new meaning. Some pain can be cloaked in poetry, wrapped in layers of words that shield it from the cold around it. The enchantment may not last long, maybe just a few moments, but it is possible.

In those rare moments, Fiamma picks up a pen and starts to write. She enjoys composing phrases on scraps of paper that she then inevitably tears up, loses, burns, or crumples up so she can forget them. Even now, she's doodling on a piece of paper with a pencil. First, she sketches a few random squiggles without meaning, then a word, and finally, a string of sentences, one after the other, like pearls on a necklace. After a while, she feels a bit better, almost happy: a prisoner, yet free; an unarmed soldier facing a legion of words.

Metal hands grip skin like a railing,
searching for a warmth that isn't there,
in an embrace that can never be.
A crooked smile bites the cold silence
of the building, lost in thought.
I stare into my coffee
and drink the night away.
Loneliness becomes a soluble companion,
one that dissolves, stains teeth,
and burns the tip of a silent tongue.
Prisoner of a legion of words,
yet still free,
the mind gnaws at the heart,
keeping it from looking down
at the flannel of the pajamas,
while decency keeps it from hoping.
The balcony railing returns
to the hands the duty
of tucking in blankets
to light and egoism.
Metal hands caress the last rapt delusion
and shove it under the pillow,
tucked away at the bottom of the bed,
waiting for the umpteenth morning.

Have you ever felt the way I feel, Dad? A prisoner of a legion of words,
yet still free, liberated from everything around you? It's happened to me
countless times, since I first moved into this place, since I had to leave the

four walls where I spent too little time with you. And since I ran from the house that, after your death, became nothing but a cage of grief, a cage too large, with too many rooms.

Since then, it's been words that have kept me company. The silent ones scratched onto paper, the whispered ones at night into the pillow before I drift off to sleep, the ones sung by my favorite bands, and the ones I vomit into the toilet. Words, words, words… Words that are sentinels and liberators. Words like feathers, and words like a blowtorch. Words that burn as they warm, words that scratch as they soothe. Words like rose petals on metal grains.

They've been my companions for years, in the form of lies and unspoken phrases. Some hang in my throat, like a knot, an undigested lump. Sometimes, they take the shape of deformed silences, other times, they stretch long and sharp, like the fingers I shove in my mouth to hold back a scream, but which, in the end, unleash the worst of them.

I wonder what you would've done in my place, Dad. And what you would've done if you could have protected me. I wonder what you think about all this, about these things I write on this imaginary paper, arabesques that no one will ever decode.

I watch myself live from the outside, as if it were you watching me, and I describe my life on bodiless letters that can't be folded, crumpled, or touched.

I'm giving you the only thing that matters to me, the only thing no one can take away. I'm giving you my words, soaked in tears and silence. My words, across the distance that separates us, beyond my fears and limits. Words. Words above everything else. Words that are something more. Words that, in the end, are just words.

Strewn with countless, tiny, barely noticeable cracks. This is how Fiamma sees the apartment she lives in.

It's full of invisible cracks, just like her heart.

In each of these minuscule cracks, Fiamma has hidden her dreams, and in each one, she dreams of escaping. Even if she stays exactly where she is, surrounded by boxes full of useless stuff she's never bothered to get rid of. Maybe because that way, she feels like she's always on the verge of leaving, and coming back again, stuck in a kind of limbo, suspended between what came before and what will come after, caught in the in-between. Always uncertain.

She bought her own birthday cake, and the candles. A long, thin number one, and a number nine with a big head, placed side by side like two wax soldiers. Pink wax, hardly melting, as she makes her wish. A wish that will never come true.

Today, Fiamma wrote another of the countless letters she'll never send, and that the recipient will never read, scribbled with shapes only she can understand. Another letter to her father. Today is just another day without him, just another day spent waiting for her mother to show up, with the same silly, selfish hope of a child waiting for Santa Claus at Christmas.

Today is just another time when, within these four walls, in her self-imposed isolation, Fiamma feels perfectly, hopelessly, and incurably alone. And foolish.

*

She listened to Abney Park again and again. Not like she had anything better to do. Well, no, she did have something to do: she was supposed to meet her mom for lunch. But her mom canceled their monthly appointment for the third time in a row, even today, on Fiamma's birthday. She didn't even bother to call. She sent a message saying she was sorry, but *something came up* and once again, she just couldn't spare any of her precious time for Fiamma.

Hey, kiddo, how are you? Hope everything's good! ☺ Can't make it today, something came up ☹ Maybe next week. I'll make it up to you, promise. HAPPY BIRTHDAY! XOXO, Mom

Fiamma frowns. How ironic that her mom thinks she's so young she can get away with using happy and sad emojis.

Sure, Mom… no problem… So sorry something-came-up-sad-emoji… It's okay. Your daughter is just here listening to steampunk music and wanting to die on her birthday. But it's fine. You're busy after all, I get it.

Fiamma would like to be brave enough to answer back for once, just to see her mom's reaction. But she can't. It takes her several minutes just to find the courage to send a message to her super-busy, always-making-herself-known, popular-on-and-off-the-stage mom. Her mom is super-busy running away from anything that isn't her own image, or the glorification of it. Super-busy forgetting that she's a mom.

Half an hour later, Fiamma's message is completely different from the one she wanted to send.

Don't worry, Mom. No problem. I'll go to Eli's for lunch. We're going shopping later anyway. We can celebrate my birthday next week!

The only thing that makes Fiamma feel a little better is knowing she'll see Elife soon. When they're together, nothing else matters, or maybe it's just that she feels like she can face her problems differently. Yes, Eli will be with her soon, and everything will be better.

*

Fiamma remembers her first time well.

It was one night, years ago, when she broke down crying in the bathroom.

The door was locked, even though no one was home. Because, well, you never know… Because some things are better done behind closed doors, to keep everything out. All of it out.

She remembers her sobs escaping her, hollow, senseless, a mess of vowels and saliva mixed with tears. She remembers how full her stomach was, after overeating. She can't remember why, or how she started eating everything in sight, endless amounts; but she remembers the discomfort of being overstuffed afterward, her stomach painfully bloated, like a balloon about to burst. And she remembers the exact moment. The start of it all. The moment when she decided to put two fingers in her mouth and purge.

That's when it started. When she realized her throat could easily play the game of life and death. Up and down like a yo-yo.

It was so easy back then. Too easy.

The hard part came later, each time she did it again, promising herself it would be the last time.

Years later, and here she is, sitting in front of her birthday cake. A beautiful cake made by her favorite baker. Layers of sponge cake – flour, eggs, butter, sugar, milk, egg whites, vanilla extract – and tons of whipped cream piled on top like soft, white snow.

They'd even put little candy roses on it, and the words 'Happy Birthday Fiamma' in chocolate. A whole cake, just for her. Every child's dream. Something delicious to eat, except for the pink wax candles, left untouched at the corner of the table like tiny, deformed limbs. Insignificant, useless.

Happy birthday to me, and a whole cake just for me.

Two fingers in her mouth, and her wish gets swallowed down the toilet in a simple flush. The whirl of clear water wrapping the pure white cream in a liquid embrace, with a touch of color here and there, like a flawed palette, making a distorted sound that her mind transforms into a song, out of tune and out of time.

For she's a jolly good fellaaaaa…that nobody can deny!

She feels light now, like the dust particles she sometimes sees floating in the air during her lessons at school. Her stomach is completely empty now. There's a void inside her that no one could fill, ever. It's like, inside that bowl, she lost the little will to live she had left. All she wants now is to disappear. That's all she really wants. Really, truly wants. No, it's more of a need. To die on her birthday. Original, ridiculous, and absurd all at once. Fiamma thinks she could easily leave right now, and nothing would change outside. It would still be March 21st. The first day of spring. The sun would still be shining, even though it's paler now compared to this morning. There would still be flowers about to bloom and flowers already bloomed. There would still be wisteria on the roof of the house across from hers with its pale violet fingers. There would still be the ringing bells of the nearby church. Everything would remain exactly and perfectly the same. As if nothing had happened. She could leave this very minute, and the world outside wouldn't make a sound. Her mother's life would probably remain the same. The beautiful, extraordinary, charming, and magnificent Sara would likely go on without missing a beat. She'd get over her daughter's departure just like she got over her dear husband's, shedding a few tears just to keep moving on with her merry way. *The show must go on*, they say, forever and ever; and those who are left behind shed a few tears and then move on with their lives. The ones left behind keep playing their roles.

I have no idea how much time has passed since I started staring at the ceiling. Maybe a thousand seconds, then another hundred. All I know is that I'm still here, my hand on my stomach, just a few millimeters away from my chest. I've been listening to the rapid beats of my heart, mixing with the involuntary rumbles of my stomach. Waves of disordered, useless contractions, pulling in stomach acid and emptiness. Energy that's gone to waste, pushing toward nothing. I don't even know how long I've been like this, how long I've been living this miserable life, filling it with my own vomit. How long I've been waiting here, hoping it'll somehow be too late. Too late for anything. Too late, as always. Too late for everything.

SARA

Sometimes life can be deeply disappointing. It turns out to be nothing like what you expected. It follows its own script, full of lines that come at the wrong time, and plot twists that leave you breathless. Yet, just like a play, life has to go on. It must continue. That's how it's always been, and how it should be. This is why there are always understudies, people who step in when the lead actor can't be there… the stand-ins. The show goes on, even without the leading lady, because what matters is the story, the plot, the narrative. And the story must always be told, no matter what. Even when the ending is absurd, when it doesn't make sense, or when it's too sad to hear, to act, to live, whether you're on stage or in the audience.

That's another reason why I love the theater, just like I love life, and have never stopped loving it, even after Daniel's death.

I've often been criticized by family and friends for how easily I rebuilt my life after he passed away.

Only a few months of mourning… too few… what a scandal, it's unbelievable! She sure got over him fast!

That poor girl… what a heartless mother! What kind of example is she setting?

She probably started seeing that guy before her husband even passed away…

What do you expect from an actress? She cares more about her career and her looks than her family…

What a scandal, what a disgrace!

And to top it off, she got involved with a theater producer, the sly thing!

People have said all sorts of things behind my back, and sometimes right to my face. But I couldn't care less. It's my life, and I'll live it the way I choose. It's the only script I can pretend to write on my own. At least for a while.

Giorgio has been my lifeline in the storm. And even though I don't love him and never will love him like I loved my husband, I need him to keep feeling alive. To keep acting in the play that someone else has written for me, and of which I still don't know the ending. Giorgio is like the understudy, who will never be as good as the lead he's replacing, but who's necessary, in one way or another. And I know, somehow, I have to be grateful to him.

I first fell in love with fire when I was fourteen. I was on vacation with my parents on Boracay Island in the Philippines, a small tropical paradise with beautiful white sandy beaches. I remember spending hours sifting sand through my fingers, watching the tiny grains of sand cascade in the light. I loved watching them fall quickly, as if they were escaping from my hands. I looked at the pink of my skin, the white of the sand, the blue of the sea and the sky beyond my hand, and in those moments, I imagined fragments of my future life and pieces of dreams.

At night, while my mother was asleep, I would walk along the beach with my father, watching the many street performers who worked outside the bars and clubs. As soon as the sun set, the strip of sand in front of our resort became an open-air stage. Under an imaginary tent full of stars, in front of tourists from all over the world, one incredible performance followed the next. That's when I fell in love with fire, when I saw a boy just a few years older than me performing spectacular feats with flaming spheres and chains. He handled the flames like they were nothing, twirling them in the air with a speed and skill I had never seen before. I fell in love with him and with every spark of light, with the kind of painful enthusiasm that only teenagers can experience. I thought about that night on the beach in Boracay for months after I came home.

I remember the day I first met Daniel like it was yesterday. A couple of friends introduced us at a party I reluctantly went to after Chiara, my classmate, insisted. The first thing he told me was his name. The second thing he said was that he was a fire-eater, performing in the streets. The third thing he told me was that he was only going to be in town for a few days.

He ended up staying for years. The best years of my life, and his too, I believe. It would be impossible to describe the happiness of that time. It would be like trying to put a sunset into words. How do you describe the touch, the smell, the sound, or the taste of it? A sunset holds all five senses, even though we only see it with our eyes. It wraps around you, takes hold of you, and draws you into a whirl of sensations that you can't help but love. Daniel was the same. People fell in love with him instinctively, almost against their will. It happened to my parents too, even though he was far from the son-in-law they had imagined. My father was the one who resisted the most, trying everything to convince me to stop seeing a guy who had very little to offer in terms of material wealth. But in the end, he gave in and accepted our love.

I went to Boracay again with Daniel, this time for our

honeymoon. It was a gift from my relatives, a gift I probably never thanked them enough for, because without knowing it, they had closed a circle that had been opened years before.

I was already a couple of months pregnant but hadn't told anyone. I decided to keep that secret to myself for a while, to let it grow inside me along with the tiny life I was carrying. Looking back, I can't even explain why. Maybe it was superstition, or maybe a small act of selfishness, wanting something so beautiful just for myself. Sometimes, while Daniel was sleeping, I would touch my belly and whisper, "When you're out of here, I'll have to share you with the world… but for now, it's just you and me… for now, we belong to each other. You're safe inside me, and I'll always be there for you, for the rest of your life."

During our vacation in Boracay, Daniel took me parasailing. It was traumatic. I was terrified, for myself and for the baby, but I couldn't say no. His enthusiasm was enough to move mountains, and it won me over, stirring my natural curiosity.

I remember exactly how I felt when we were lifted ten meters above the ocean, held up by what seemed like a very flimsy harness. It was a feeling of total powerlessness. I felt completely at the mercy of the situation, completely dependent on a small group of people waiting on an old boat, probably more interested in our wallets than in our safety. I felt helpless and vulnerable.

I only felt something similar, but much worse, once more in my life: when I found out Daniel had stomach cancer. His illness became part of our daily lives, and it drained away his strength, physical and emotional, devouring the man I had once thought of as invincible.

The day I got the call from the hospital, I was at my parents' house. My mother answered the phone. It was a beautiful May day, windy but sunny, and she had just picked cherries from the tree in the garden. I can still picture her face, red from the sun and the effort, her left hand holding the corner of her apron full of cherries. I remember her face turning paler than the apron, and the cherries falling to the ground, like big, blood-red hailstones.

"For Pete's sake, Fiamma! You're always late! Hurry up and come down!"

Elife's frustrated, slightly irritated voice coming through the intercom has become a familiar tune in the background of their friendship. Eli's impatience always seems to rouse Fiamma from her moments of stupor and emptiness, saving her from her self-destructive thoughts with the urgency of her presence, demanding the attention she needs.

Fiamma struggles with time. She's hopeless when it comes to being punctual. Elife, however, is perpetually early; she shows up at least fifteen minutes ahead of every appointment. It's hard to understand why she insists on arriving early for meetings with Fiamma, especially since she knows full well that Fiamma will never be on time, and it means waiting at least twenty minutes.

As usual, Fiamma hesitates for a moment before finally deciding to finish getting dressed and leave the house. She often stands in front of the mirror for several minutes, lost in her own reflection. More often than not, she feels an overwhelming urge to just stay home, lock the world out, and retreat into herself. But once Elife rings the doorbell again, she shakes herself from the stupor, quickly puts on her favorite black steamer boots – the ones with clock parts on the sides – grabs her bag, and heads out the door, ready to escape her loneliness, or at least pretend to.

The air outside is cool and refreshing, filled with the scents of spring. Fiamma thinks she can smell the wisteria growing on the roof of the building across from her apartment. For a brief moment, she forgets all the sadness from the morning, the endless waiting for her mother who never showed up, the emptiness she felt after vomiting, the long hours spent staring at the ceiling.

She hugs Elife, planting two big kisses on her cheeks, greeting her with an enthusiasm that brightens her face with a radiant, photogenic smile.

"I wasn't that late this time!" she says, her voice as innocent as a child caught in the act of mischief.

Elife has a special ability to make her feel better in an instant, no matter what has happened or how Fiamma feels at the moment. She is truly happy to see her, as she always is. In fact, she considers this to be the best birthday gift she's received today.

"You're right, birthday girl, only 9 minutes and 40 seconds late this time. Maybe you're getting better…"

Elife smiles with a teasing, mockingly stern look, as though she has already forgiven yet another delay. She grabs Fiamma's hand firmly, as if pulling her away from the emptiness that surrounds her, pulling her into herself. Anyone who saw them together would probably think they were sisters, given how much they look alike, despite their completely different styles. Same height, same body type, same length of hair. The only difference is that Elife's hair is black, not red, and she wears large, blue-framed glasses that obscure the beautiful color of her eyes without completely hiding it. They're not sisters, and they haven't known each other for long, but they share a deep connection, a connection born not only of affection but of loneliness, the kind of loneliness that has isolated them both from the world and now binds them together in friendship. Elife has no one else she truly considers a friend, other than Fiamma. She certainly doesn't count the handful of virtual acquaintances on social media as real friends. They are just names and faces on an anonymous contact list.

Fiamma, on the other hand, has an emptiness inside and around her that no one else has been able to fill. Elife is the only one who has managed to make this emptiness feel a little smaller, simply by being there. She is the only person in the world whose presence can help her feel less alone, even in silence.

*

"So, how was your brother's girlfriend's little brother's party yesterday? You didn't mention it."

Fiamma and Elife have been walking around Via del Corso for over two hours now. During this time, Elife has followed her friend around patiently, enduring the ordeal of watching Fiamma try on countless clothes and accessories, only to put them back every time.

"Well, there's not much to say. Honestly, I don't think the party was that great. Only about twenty percent of the kids even bothered to dance, and that was only after the birthday boy's mom kept insisting. Thirty percent just sat there, watching the others. And the remaining fifty percent just stuffed their faces non-stop with chips, pretzels, and sandwiches that barely had anything inside them. I tried one, and it was completely dry. Barely a slice of ham!"

"Wow… sounds like a real blast!" Fiamma jokes, grinning at her friend. Elife looks back at her with a disheartened expression. She's clearly exhausted from the shopping marathon.

"Why don't we grab tea at that little place on Via XX Settembre, you know, Cioccote or whatever it's called…" suggests Fiamma, feeling a little guilty. "I've heard it's the best in the city. And at least we can sit down for a bit… I've worn you out with this shopping spree." Elife is quick to agree, her stomach growling in agreement. They head toward Via XX Settembre, and when they reach Largo di Santa Susanna, they notice a small crowd gathered in front of the Church of Santa Maria della Vittoria. About ten or twenty people are standing in a slightly disorganized, colorful semicircle. Some are standing on the sidewalk, others spill into the street, seemingly oblivious to the chaos of speeding scooters and cars. They're all facing the same direction, staring at something.

"Do you have any idea what's going on there?"

Eli responds with a look that suggests she's contemplating the meaning of life itself: "Why are you asking me? I have no clue. But let's go see, I'm curious!" They squeeze through the crowd, moving between the gaps left by the bodies, pushing past people with disapproving looks and muttering comments, until they finally make it to the front row. And that's when they discover the source of all the attention: a street performer, a young man in his twenties, sitting on a small wooden stool, playing a series of glass bottles of varying sizes, filled with different amounts of water. He taps the bottles with two felt-tipped mallets, making them resonate like the bars of a vibraphone, and the result is incredible.

Fiamma and Elife watch in awe as his hands move quickly from one bottle to the next. They are mesmerized, like the rest of the crowd, listening to the melodies that emerge from the watery vibrations of the glass, a blend of wood, felt, and pure magic.

"Wow, every note is spot on… it's incredible! Look at his

hands!" Eli says, full of awe. Her muffled voice reaches Fiamma through a kind of haze, from somewhere far, far away, and it's a little annoying. Fiamma shuts it out, focusing on the music. She pushes Eli's voice into the background, blending with the murmurs of the people around her, people she's already dismissed. She doesn't make a sound, but her head moves just slightly to the rhythm, her gaze fixed on the strange boy, completely spellbound. What draws her in isn't the way his hands move so quickly over the mallets, almost like extensions of his body, nor the flawless flow of notes that follow one after the other. It's not even the music filling the air, swallowing up everything around her, even the sounds of traffic, honking horns, engines, and screeching brakes. Standing there, in the middle of the crowd that's become shapeless and colorless, Fiamma finds herself drawn to the boy's face, his intense expression. Even though he's about her age, he seems so much older, almost like an adult in contrast to her and everyone else around them, light-years away from the people following his fingers' movements, flesh meeting wood. It's as if he's playing just for himself, not for the audience that's gathered. Maybe he's playing for someone who isn't even here, someone far away, or maybe someone who doesn't exist at all, except in his mind. Fiamma takes in his black, curly hair framing his oval face. He has an olive complexion, large, slightly almond-shaped eyes that seem to change color. She studies his small, straight nose, his serious mouth, which occasionally hints at a smile, the tiny dimple in his right cheek, a sign of the shyness he hides behind the confident front he puts on as he performs for this impromptu crowd. She watches every inch of him, every movement of his body.

The boy lifts his eyes from the bottles and glances at the audience, flashing a smile like a seasoned performer. But his eyes, his eyes don't match the smile. They seem to be looking through the crowd, beyond them, as if searching for something. Fiamma wishes she could believe that maybe his eyes rested on her face for more than just a second. For a moment, she has the feeling he's looking straight at her, and not absently, like with the others. His smile, too, seems different now, less rehearsed, less impersonal, more intimate. That's when she notices the color of his eyes: a strange shade, almost amber, but she can't be entirely sure because the sun is so bright and she's standing so far away.

"He's smiling at me," Fiamma thinks, not saying anything to Eli. She stays serious but smiles back at him, shyly. "That smile isn't just for some random face in the crowd. He's not staring blankly in front of him at nothing. That smile is for me. Just for me." She repeats this to herself as she watches the boy's eyes and hands, as she watches the mallets, wooden, felt-tipped, twirl in his hands, and hears the bottles and the water inside them vibrate. It's all for me. Just for me. Like my birthday cake. Everything is for her. That's how Fiamma interprets his unreadable amber gaze as it sweeps over the disorganized, multi-colored crowd that has gathered there by chance, a brief pause in their chaotic lives. It's all for her. Just for her.

I'm still thinking about that boy, Dad. The street performer who was sitting in front of the church, playing his water bottles. Our eyes met for just a second, and yet it feels like I've known him forever. Maybe I'm overthinking it, and he wasn't even looking at me. Maybe his eyes just happened to briefly glance at mine as he surveyed the crowd that had gathered around him, and he didn't even notice me. Maybe to him, I was just another anonymous face lost among the other anonymous faces watching him. Who knows? Maybe I'm just daydreaming like I always do, building castles in the air like when I was little, and you'd tell me that no dream was ever a waste, that it's always worth dreaming. Did you really believe that, Dad? You said so many things when I was little, just to make me happy. You were my Santa Claus, my Tooth Fairy, my Befana, and my Mister Neverwhere, who I still remember so well. You created him just for me, and now I know that no other little girl had a Mister Neverwhere. You told me he was a little man who gave children gifts when he saw they had lost hope, even for just a moment, that there was more to life than what you could see and touch. I remember every one of those gifts so perfectly: you gave me a kite with my picture on it when I said you couldn't fly just with your imagination; a huge seashell inside a pail when I said you couldn't catch the sea; a little book with all kinds of poems written by countless poets when I said you couldn't change the world with words; and a CD with sounds that were strange and indecipherable, yet somehow marvelous, when I said that silence was the best kind of noise. I miss Mister Neverwhere so much, Dad. If you were still here, do you know what I'd ask you — or rather, what I'd ask Him — sitting on your lap in the evening before bed? I'd ask where all my smiles have gone, where my will to live and be happy has disappeared. A few nights ago, I went to bed with that thought in my head. And I imagined waking up to find a collage of all the pictures of me smiling as a little girl, surrounded by people who are smiling too, like in some magical mirror. I wonder if Mister Neverwhere really exists somewhere in the world, or if he died with you that day.

If her mother doesn't cancel again this time, Fiamma and Sara will meet this afternoon for their usual recap of what's been going on in their lives. Every now and then, they remember they're mother and daughter (or rather, Sara remembers she has a daughter) and get together to talk about what's happened in the past few days. It's a sort of small tradition they've kept up for a year now, ever since Fiamma moved out to live on her own, just after turning 18. She left home the minute she could, literally running away from the nightmare of living with her mother and Giorgio.

They're meeting at 5, but Fiamma's already been waiting for a quarter of an hour in their favorite café, like an impatient lover. She's already ordered their usual: cinnamon tea for herself and pineapple juice for Sara. No sugar, of course.

The café is half full, with customers, voices, and the sound of porcelain and glasses clinking. Everyone seems lost in their own thoughts, though some are pretending to listen to the person sitting next to them. As soon as Sara walks through the door, everything stops, suspended in the air for a second. Every sound, every word, every thought freezes for a moment. That's the effect Sara has. Every time she enters a room, she commands attention. It's the way her hair moves when she walks, her slow, almost deliberate pace, her allure, her scent. She's impossible to ignore. She's an actress, after all, and Fiamma believes she's just as much of an actress off-stage as on. Sara knows how to make sure all eyes are on her.

When she sees Fiamma, Sara beams and theatrically waves at her, raising her right arm in a grand gesture. Fiamma responds with a simple lift of four fingers on her left hand, resting on the table.

Fiamma feels agitated, nervous, and unsure in her chair. She's always like this around her mother. She sits on the edge of her chair, feet planted on the floor, legs slightly apart, hands gripping the edge of the table, her butt barely touching the seat. It's as if she's ready to get up and leave. Sara, on the other hand, is perfectly calm, exuding an almost unreachable perfection, beautiful beyond belief. Fiamma reflects that her mother has always been stunning, with angelic features and a mass of fiery red hair. Even now, past forty, she still shines with the same radiance she had at twenty. Nothing on her face is out of place. Her body is an anthem to beauty. *She's always flawless, and I'm always so messy*, Fiamma thinks with a mix of resignation and sadness.

As she steals a glance at their reflection in the mirror behind the bar, Fiamma notices how far from perfection she herself is. She shares her mother's red hair, but lacks those striking emerald green eyes, large, almond-shaped, and bright as a movie star's. Hers are dark, like coal, with slightly heavy lids, as if perpetually tired. Her upper lip is fuller than her lower lip, giving her a permanent pout. Her nose is small, like Sara's, but slightly crooked, making it imperfect. Her skin is fair, almost milky white, sensitive to the sun. Meanwhile, Sara's skin… Her skin glows like raw sugar crystals when light shines through them.

"Well, finally!" are Sara's first words after settling in. Her diva act immediately draws the attention of everyone in the café. Fiamma wants to reply, pointing out how that the word *finally* seems misplaced, like it's her fault they haven't seen each other in forever, like she was the one who canceled their last three plans. Instead, she just purses her lips, a grimace of pain more than a smile.

"Yeah… finally!"

She doesn't say more, trying not to meet her mother's eyes. She focuses on a distant point, somewhere even she can't quite place.

"Go on, tell me something!"

Fiamma has always hated this line. What does "tell me something" even mean? What is Sara really asking for? A fairy tale? A novel? A science fiction story? What's the point of *telling something*? For Fiamma, it's a vague, silly request, kind of like 'what's new with you?'

"Aren't you going to answer me?" Sara insists. "Come on, tell me, what's new with you?"

Exactly.

"Mamma, what do you want me to say? Honestly, nothing's going on. I don't really have anything exciting to share." She shifts in her seat, trying to balance the pressure of her legs against the slippery plastic.

"Fiamma, you're such a pessimist! I refuse to believe that at 19 you haven't had anything worth sharing! When I was your age, every day was a new surprise…"

"Mom, please… Don't start with that again," Fiamma pleads, not wanting to hear the 'when I was your age' speech.

"But I'm just trying to help! We barely see each other, and every time you're so sad, so angry at the world. It's absurd. How can there be nothing good in your life? Your birthday was just a few days ago… Surely you celebrated with a friend? You're still so young, Fiamma… Maybe all you need is a good guy to make you happy. You never talk about any guys. Don't you want to open up to me? I can't believe you've never had a boyfriend, you're so beautiful…"

"Oh, please!" Fiamma interrupts, fed up with the flood of clichés. "Being pretty doesn't mean you have a line of guys chasing after you. Ever thought that maybe I have such a terrible personality that no one wants to be around me? Or that people think I'm too weird, too different to hang out with? Or that my life has been such a mess that it's hard for me to connect with anyone?"

She only realizes she's gone too far after she's spoken. And when she notices the raised volume of her voice, she sees the other café customers turning to look at them in surprise.

"Fiamma…"

Her name sounds like a plea from Sara's lips. She's begging her not to shout, but, mostly, she's begging her not to throw the truth in her face, the truth Sara's been desperately hiding from herself, from her daughter, and from the world for years.

The truth is that since Daniel died, they haven't been a family anymore.

The truth is that since he left, a void has formed between them. His absence carved out a chasm that divided them, locking them each in their own ivory tower, two princesses trapped in their sorrow and loneliness.

Sara's eyes beg her not to speak the truth, not like this, not now, not here.

They beg Fiamma to act, to perform in life as Sara does on stage. Sara is pleading for Fiamma to pretend, to lie, because it's easier this way. It hurts less, and life seems more beautiful, even when it's a total mess. Pretend and lie, that's her solution. And they lived happily ever after. Amen.

For once, Fiamma decides to play along, at least to make her mother happy. For once, she decides to step onto the stage and act. After all, it can't be that hard.

She stares into her mother's eyes for a second, then forces a smile. "You're right. Something did happen recently…"

Pretend and lie.

"I met someone I really like…"

In an instant, Sara's eyes and face light up so brightly that Fiamma is encouraged to continue without feeling guilty at all. Her mother is radiating happiness now, glowing with this joy that has suddenly blossomed around her. She's even more beautiful than usual, so much so that Fiamma can't help but be fascinated. For the first time in a while, Fiamma finds herself energized by this new light, this newfound joy. She decides to feed off it, to live in this false reality. After all, Fiamma is just as skilled at pretending.

Pretend and lie. That's the answer. The easiest choice.

And Fiamma keeps pretending, keeps lying, once again to please her mother, or at least to protect her from the truth. Whether it helps or not doesn't matter, not now, at least. Fiamma soaks in the light she sees growing on her mother's face and draws strength from it to continue her web of lies. And, in her story, the artist she met while out with Elife, whose name she doesn't even know, becomes a guy she's been seeing for almost a month now. A *boyfriend*, as Sara would call him… such a silly, outdated term. A boyfriend who's handsome, sweet, funny, and full of talent. Most importantly, he's showered her with attention. Sara listens, not saying a word, as they both build, piece by piece, the story of a perfect little world, just for Sara's eyes and ears. The world Fiamma is creating only to make her happy. Piece by piece, it becomes a whole world, more and more elaborate with each word. And for once, Sara is genuinely pleased, lost in the fairy tale Fiamma is telling. Pretend and lie. And they lived happily ever after.

Amen.

*

She returns home feeling even emptier than before. Lying can drain you more than telling the truth. It's something Fiamma learned during her years of struggling with bulimia. It's a truth she came to grips with soon after her father's death, when her mother began dating her new boyfriend, a substitute father figure she's never been able to accept or recognize as such.

She comes back holding a gift bag she hasn't even opened, along with the stack of cash he sent through her mother to cover her rent, groceries, bills, and hopefully ease his own conscience just a little.

Her fist clenches around that crumpled piece of paper, worthless except for the ink smeared across it. The same fist that she never threw at him, or at the mess that has surrounded her life for so long.

She returns home with an invitation she never wanted to receive: a dinner with him and her mother to celebrate the fact that she's *finally* in love. And a birthday that's already passed.

Years ago, yet it feels like today. I keep reliving it. I am living it right now. It has never ended. It has never really stopped.

His shiny black boots, with just a tiny speck of dirt on the heel of the left one. His black boots that kick my lucid mind, the memory of it, the memory of that moment that has never really passed. Expanded into an endless present, comfortably stretching towards the future. His boots scraping against the darkness of a night many years ago, a night that now seems so different from the one I see floating outside my window. His adult boots, through my child's eyes. The same boots I saw him wear the next day, and the day after that, boots I could never bring myself to look up at. His shiny black adult boots that crushed my childhood nights and my adolescent dreams, that silently smashed down the door to my womanhood, and for years, trampled on the echo of my fear. His silent boots crept toward my bed, commanding me in clipped words to stay silent.

"Be a good girl, or you'll wake your mom. Be quiet, and nothing will happen. Good girls always obey, always."

Always. Always, in my mind, those words. Always, in my mind, those black boots before my eyes. Those boots I saw by my bed, growing blurry in my tear-filled gaze, floating in the wet silence of shame and disgust. His boots forever in and out of my bedroom door, by my bed, in those seconds that stretched on forever.

"Be a good girl, and nothing will happen. It won't hurt. Your mom took her pills, she's sleeping soundly. Don't wake her. You don't want to wake her, do you? This is our secret. Good girls keep secrets."

I've been a good girl for years and have kept our secret. I kept it hidden under the dark blankets that those black boots would always awkwardly pull up before slipping away, out the door, crushing the silence.

Mom is still sleeping soundly, somewhere outside this door, in another house.

I fall asleep staring at the door, terrified it might open suddenly. And I hate the shiny black of every night, a hatred that has haunted me for so many years.

SMOKE

She tears off a piece of bread from the wicker basket in the center of the table and shoves it into her mouth without chewing. A bit of crust scrapes her throat before sliding down her esophagus. She senses her mom's disapproval before she even opens her mouth:

"Don't stuff yourself with bread, Fiamma. You're going to ruin your appetite!"

Poor thing, she has no idea where that tiny piece of flour and water, along with the meal they're about to eat, will end up. She doesn't realize that there's no way a measly piece of bread will ruin her appetite.

Fiamma lifts her eyes and shakes her head quickly, forcing a smile. She already has everything planned in her mind, even before sitting down to dinner, before stepping into the restaurant, even before leaving the house: as soon as Sara and Giorgio ask for the check, she'll go to the bathroom. With all the water and wine she drank, it's just going to run right through her. She'll joke, "Not even twenty, and I'm already incontinent. Can you imagine when I'm old?"

Fiamma has figured out that any silly comment, no matter how stupid, gives you the freedom to do what you want, like leaving the table before the meal is even finished. It's a distraction, a way to break the awkward silence that always falls when two or more people are together for no clear reason.

"Don't worry, I barely ate today. There's no way that little bit of bread is going to ruin my appetite... I'll eat everything on my plate, like always, you'll see!"

Giorgio nods and smiles with the look of someone just trying to end the evening. "Leave her alone, Sara. The service here isn't exactly fast. It's going to take a while before we get our food."

Fiamma hates it when Giorgio defends her because she knows he's only doing it to feel less guilty and uncomfortable when they're together. He's scared of her, and he's been paying for her silence for years, both with money and by defending her. So in front of everyone, especially Sara, he looks magnanimous, tolerant, and generous, the kind of guy who can understand and even make excuses for a teenager who's not even his daughter.

Fiamma lets him do it because it benefits her, but she ends up hating herself, him, his money, and his guilt.

The restaurant is one of those places famous for tiny portions and sky-high prices, and, of course, the wine list is ten times longer than the menu. It's one of those pretentious spots where waiters, with their ridiculous bow ties and clingy plastic uniforms, bring out giant white plates with tiny, colorful amounts of food. And they do it all with such a serious face, they almost look pissed off. Of course, Giorgio picked the place, because he loves showing off and flaunting his wealth, just like he loves sitting at the *Reserved* table, even when the place is practically empty. But what he loves most is knowing that all eyes are on him, watching how everyone reacts. When he walks in with Sara on his arm, dressed in his perfect Patrick Bateman *American Psycho* suit, he sparks envy in older men and desire in older women, and then, it flips: desire in older men and envy in older women.

The crowd here is just like you'd expect: super fancy guys in tuxedos, and women in evening dresses fresh from the salon. Everyone, no matter their gender, is doused in expensive perfume, like they're saying, 'My pee is champagne-colored, not straw yellow!'

Fiamma adjusts her chair, inching it closer to the edge of the table, then moves it back, only to repeat the motion again. She does it quickly and nervously, but in complete silence. When she's out to eat with Giorgio and her mom, she can never seem to find the right distance between herself and the table, or the right posture. Her movements are almost imperceptible, balancing carefully on the four legs of the chair. Every now and then, someone will catch her fidgeting, staring at her with curiosity mixed with a little disgust, as though she's some rare animal just discovered. Clearly, her steampunk outfit, with its long frilly skirt, Victorian goth corset, goggles, top hat, and boots with brass clock gears on the sides, makes an impression.

Giorgio asks the waiter for a 2009 Brunello, a bottle of sparkling water, and three orders of filet mignon with Grappa and blackberry sauce. He's always the first to order; Sara follows his lead like a loyal puppy, and Fiamma just follows both of them because she's too lazy to pick something else. Roasted potatoes, seasonal vegetables, and a cup of raspberries for dessert to round out the meal.

Fiamma eats almost in total silence, devouring the food, nodding every so often without ever lifting her head from her plate. She pretends to listen to her mom and Giorgio, but does her best to avoid meeting Giorgio's gaze, even though she can feel it on her.

The few times she lifts her head, she looks at her mom's face, her green eyes and red lipstick, or, distractedly, at Giorgio's hands gesturing nonstop. She focuses on the bottles on the table or the heads of the other diners, barely moving above their plates. She mixes the conversations at her table with snippets from nearby tables, familiar voices blending with strangers' words.

"I don't think choosing Carlo for Hamlet was a good idea; he can't really get into character..."
"Want some more wine?"
"What are you in the mood for? What should we order?"
"You'd better think twice before accusing me for no reason next time!"
"He's perfect for it, I think. He's young, troubled..."
"Should we ask for the bill?"
"This place isn't as good as the one we usually go to... Don't you think the tables are too close together? There's such a thing as privacy..."
"You were right, the service is slow here..."
"Federico will never measure up to his brother. He'll never make it, no matter how hard he tries."
"Did you see what that girl is wearing? Ridiculous..."
"Black really suits you, my dear..."
"You know, kids today are all so strange... rebellious..."
"This place used to be so exclusive. Now they let anyone in."
"Another work trip? You're always gone these days!"
"We need to pay the private investigator who's keeping tabs on Sandro this month..."
"This filet is delicious, isn't it? So tender."

Fiamma finishes her meal in a matter of minutes. The filet's gone in seconds, the potatoes are inhaled almost instantly, the vegetables barely touched, and the Brunello is gulped down, without a word or even a chance to savor it, although judging by Giorgio's face, it must be excellent. She only speaks when the dessert arrives, and her mom, noticing her appetite, asks how school is going. Fiamma gives a half-hearted answer as the yogurt and cream mix into a sweet cloud in her mouth.

"Nothing new. Same old, same old."

The words, the sweetness of the dessert, and the bitter desire to escape all blend together.

Giorgio's the smart one, or maybe just the slick one. He never asks her anything personal, and most of the time, he talks directly to her mom. He's not dumb, he knows that's the only sensible thing to do. Stay out of her way, at least for now. Just leave her alone.

As soon as she finishes her dessert, Fiamma stands up to head to the bathroom.

"Excuse me for a sec... I drank too much water and wine, and I can't hold it anymore. Could you order an American coffee for me while I'm gone? I'll be back in a minute..."

*

They insisted on driving her home, even though she didn't want them to. She would've much rather taken a bus or, better yet, walked. If it were up to her, she'd walk ten miles straight to avoid spending even five minutes in Giorgio's fancy car. He treats that car like a shrine. It's always spotless, inside and out, as if it just rolled off the showroom floor. Giorgio likes everything around him to be perfectly in order, exactly how he wants it, under control. His control.

Sara got out of the car with her daughter, to give her one last kiss. She stood there staring at her for a moment in silence, with a proud and satisfied smile, while Fiamma couldn't help but wonder what she was thinking, what she was seeing, or pretending to see as she looked at her. Then she hugged her and planted a kiss on her right cheek. Fiamma felt the sticky residue of her lipstick and instinctively closed her eyes for a moment. She inhaled her mother's perfume – overly sweet as usual, a mix of vanilla and floral notes – and after just a second, she pulled away abruptly, muttering a barely audible good night.

"See you, Mom…"

"Bye, baby girl. Take care of yourself… and study!"

As Fiamma shut the apartment building's front door, she watched her mother get into the car, noticing that the hem of her dress had gotten caught in the car door without her noticing. "Always in such a hurry and so careless," Fiamma mumbled, standing still as she watched the fluttering piece of cotton fabric, swept away by the wind and Giorgio's speeding car.

Now that she's alone, she doesn't have to lie anymore. She can be herself again, free to be or not be, to speak or stay silent, and to purge everything that doesn't sit right with her. She locks the door behind her, leaving the world outside, outside of the heavy wooden door with the double lock. She can finally hide in her ivory tower like a sad princess who chooses to shut herself off from everything. Whoever's inside is inside, and whoever's outside is outside. Inside, there's just her, a playlist full of steampunk tracks and some goth albums on her phone, and a pack of cigarettes. Outside, there's a whole bunch of opportunities that she has neither the desire nor the energy to face. A whole series of paths she's not willing to walk, emotions she just can't feel.

She's never told anyone her secret. It's a secret even bigger and darker than her bulimia, something far harder to speak about. It's a secret that makes her feel filthier than all the days spent hunched over a toilet, emptying her stomach until her esophagus aches, until her knuckles are torn up from her teeth, until her eyes bulge out of their sockets, bloodshot and filled with all the horrors they've had to witness.

That secret tainted her deeply a long time ago, marking her soul irreparably with vomit. Sometimes, she wished she could keep that secret even from herself. And for years, she managed to, by burying the memory. Suddenly, he stopped coming to her room. To her bed. It happened after Fiamma finally found the courage to look him straight in the eye and spit out all the hate she'd felt, all the rage built up over years of suffering and endurance.

"You disgust me, and one day you'll pay for this."

She said it simply. A few words, but all of them packed with the full weight of the hatred she'd been carrying. She fired the words out in one breath, her eyes locked on him like the barrel of a gun. Ten words, like ten commandments, like ten bullets fired straight from her mouth, one after the other. Her childlike eyes had suddenly turned cruel and adult. No longer the innocent, terrified, lost gaze she had a moment ago, but two coals, burning with only one purpose: to burn away his desire, to destroy the lust in his eyes as he lay on top of her, her body pressed down against the cotton sheets.

After that night, his hands never touched her again.

After that night, Fiamma's door stayed closed, as did her mouth and her heart. And for a few years after that last night, she was able to keep that memory wrapped in thick layers, hidden deep in her mind, determined to forget it. For a while, it worked. Sometimes the memory tried to break through the layers of forgetfulness she'd wrapped it in, but she always managed to push it back, out of sight, away from her awareness. Until... until one day, Fiamma could no longer lie to herself. Until she decided to bring it to light, to expel it from her body like a piece of undigested food, to drag it out of her insides, to vomit it up with her hands and free herself from it once and for all. That act became a ritual for her: she fills the emptiness left by years of silence with food, letting it soak up all the filth inside her, and then she gets rid of it, purging it in a slurry of words and flavors down into the toilet bowl.

And all she has to do is flush. Just a push of a button, and for a moment, she can believe it's all over, that it's been completely wiped away, sucked down by a whirlpool of water and tears. Gone from sight, gone from memory.

Fiamma often thinks it would be nice if she could vomit up her heart too.

When I was really little, I was scared of the dark. The outside dark, the one that came when the lights went off. Now, I love the outside dark; I love the night, and I enjoy being in the dark or just surrounded by the flicker of a candle. The only dark I'm afraid of now is the one I carry inside, stuck to my soul like tar.

Her mother, Sara, never noticed anything, or at least that's what Fiamma believes, and mostly, what she hopes. Sara never noticed a thing, not even a hint of suspicion. She was probably too focused on herself, on staying beautiful and using that beauty to succeed. She was too absorbed by the monster of a man she'd met shortly after her husband's death, with whom she moved in almost immediately. Even though she never said it to her face, Fiamma couldn't accept how quickly her mother moved on after her father's death, or how easily she seemed to get over the pain of losing him, throwing herself into the arms of someone else. To Fiamma, it made her mother seem weak, like a shapeless chameleon who adopted the traits of whoever she was with, someone stronger, someone willing to give her all the attention she craved.

Fiamma knew her parents had met when they were very young, and it had been love at first sight. A beautiful, intense, and overwhelming love, the kind of love fairy tales are made of. They had spent months living like nomads, traveling from city to city in a caravan. Sara followed her true love everywhere, without hesitation, without complaint, never missing the material comforts she'd left behind at her parents' house. Probably, all that mattered to her was having a man by her side who made her feel desired, who made her the center of his world, who made her proud every time he performed in public spaces, in one square after another. All she needed was someone to hold her, to protect her from feeling alone. Fiamma had often heard her say how happy they were, living a carefree,

free-spirited life, bound only by their love for each other.

But after Fiamma was born, their previous life felt inadequate. They needed a real home, a proper room for their child to sleep in, a real bedroom with pink walls, a large crib, a musical butterfly mobile, and walls adorned with fluttering colors to fill her dreams.

Once, Fiamma asked her mother if her arrival had ruined their plans, making their life more mundane and forcing them into something more *normal*, maybe even something less enjoyable. The change, that shift in their life, made Fiamma feel guilty.

But Sara quickly reassured her, saying their new life was no less interesting than the one they had before. "It wasn't a change of direction, and certainly not a loss," her mother had comforted her. "If anything, your presence has made our happiness even greater."

Her birth had been an immense joy for both Daniel and Sara, right from the start. And so was the joy they felt moving into their small ground-floor apartment in an old building on the outskirts of town, not far from Sara's parents' house. A 60-square-meter rented flat, with a small garden, just 20 more square meters of land that Daniel had insisted on, so he wouldn't feel too uprooted from the life he once lived outdoors, close to nature.

In that garden, Fiamma learned about plants and animals. It was in that house that she took her first steps and spoke her first words. And it was there that she and her mother first encountered the devastating illness that would turn their world upside down.

Daniel's cancer hit them like a hurricane, devastating everything in its path, leaving them raw, exposed, and defenseless. It tore the roof off their happiness and shattered the façade of their serene life. Even though

Fiamma was very young, her parents didn't keep anything from her. They told her what was happening, and what was going to happen in the months to come. From that moment, Daniel stopped being the invincible hero in her fairy tales, someone capable of defeating dragons, and became a frail, vulnerable man, at the mercy of his illness. The strong, athletic fire-eater who could tame and swallow flames, was reduced to a pile of bones and grey skin in just a few months.

After her father's death, Fiamma withdrew into a silence that no one could penetrate. Her mother, on the other hand, responded to the grief in her own way: by trying to smother the pain. She started going out almost every night, leaving Fiamma with her grandmother. She filled the emptiness left by Daniel with new people, hundreds of faces, and thousands of words. His death exposed a side of Sara that was malleable, someone who could easily be shaped by anyone offering the illusion of pulling her away from the darkness she feared. In her grief, Sara turned to a desperate search for someone who could make her feel that she was not truly alone.

Unfortunately, that someone came in the form of a theater producer, a man who could feed her need to be admired, adored, and surrounded by attention. A man who helped her fulfill her dreams of being an actress, while indulging her endless ego.

To Fiamma's misfortune, this man turned out to be a monster disguised as a respectable person, elegantly poised, handsome, with a soothing voice.

And to Fiamma's misfortune, that man was Giorgio.

I play with fire, but I'm not a performer. I'm not like you, Dad, a fire-eater who can captivate and mesmerize. I don't have that artist's spark. I don't twirl fire in the air, or let it slide down my body, or my tongue, in front of an awestruck audience. I don't swallow it and spit it out like the dragons you used to tell me about. I don't entertain anyone. I don't have an audience. In fact, I'm careful to always close the door behind me when I do what I do after I've eaten too much. I don't want anyone to watch me. I lock the door even when I'm home alone. Even in this shitty little apartment I share with nothing but my loneliness.

My fire isn't anything like yours was. It doesn't attract the attention of dozens of people like yours did, when you stood in the middle of a square with your torch in hand, wielding it like a sword in front of a crowd of eager eyes. I remember standing off to the side, because Mom always told me to stay out of your way when you were working. I would watch you with awe, like you were some kind of hero from a storybook. You looked so huge, standing there in that circle of amber light, surrounded by small, shadowy figures. You were my dad, my very own fire-eater. And as I watched you, I knew you were different from everyone else, better than everyone else, and no one could defeat you. If you could control fire, that meant you could control life, death, and everything in between.

But I was wrong.

Life fucked you over, and death took you too soon. You were unlucky, so much more than anyone else, and I never saw it coming. Just another guy who died young from a stupid stomach cancer.

I never would've guessed it, and I still don't understand why.

Why? Why you? Why us? Why me?

Why?

I puke a whole bunch of question marks into the toilet. I see them floating there with chunks of food. I puke up the emptiness and the fire inside me, and every time, all I get in return is my own sadness, clapping back at me.

She's gone to visit her friend Blue down at the station. She calls her Blue because of the funny blue hat she always wears. Always, without fail, every minute of every day, no matter the season or weather. Fiamma has known her for a few months and has never seen her without it. She's convinced Blue sleeps with it on, that she was born wearing that odd blue hat. Fiamma doesn't even know her real name. The one time she tried to ask, Blue snapped, "What difference does it make? Why do you want to know?" and that quickly shut Fiamma up.

Blue has a strange way of speaking, when she does speak, which isn't often. She likes to sprinkle famous quotes from authors into her sentences and often speaks in a poetic style, sometimes even using rhymes and assonance. Fiamma noticed this right away, and it both baffled and entertained her. She's often wondered why she expresses herself this way. Maybe she's always been like this. Maybe something broke inside her long ago. Or maybe living in a place so steeped in misery and grime just pushed her over the edge.

To most people, Blue would likely seem unbalanced, or at least odd. But Fiamma cares for her, even admires her, like a sad court jester or someone from a faraway place no one understands. She's probably read and studied hundreds of books. Every time Fiamma sees her, she's reading something new. The books are always used, with yellowed pages and worn-out covers.

Fiamma has no idea where Blue gets the books. Ever since she made the mistake of asking her name and she snapped, she hasn't dared to ask her anything personal.

Blue lives in front of one of the cafés at the station, in a wheelchair loaded with bags hanging from both sides. There are usually five white bags of different sizes on the right and seven colored bags on the left: red, orange, yellow, green, blue, indigo, and violet. It's unclear whether this is intentional or just a coincidence that they resemble the colors of the rainbow.

Knowing Blue, it's probably just a bizarre, poetic coincidence. Occasionally, Blue will open one of those bags when Fiamma is there, revealing bits of her life: a grey blouse, probably once white; a crumpled picture of a young girl with Blue's eyes and hair, smiling like the others around her; an old heart-shaped locket with tiny photographs inside; a collection of Shakespeare's sonnets, yellowed and stained; strange objects whose purpose is unclear; and various souvenirs. All of this hangs from her wheelchair, her only means of transport and her home.

When Fiamma first saw Blue, she thought she was very old. Her face looked like a crumpled piece of paper that someone had tried to iron smooth. She was begging, waving her arms to get the attention of passersby, and cursing them if they ignored her. Sometimes, she'd bang her bags together noisily.

Fiamma had plenty of money that first day. Giorgio had recently emptied his wallet to ease his conscience. He'd given her enough for rent, food, bills, and even a little extra. She'd gone into the café, bought a cola for herself, and a sandwich and beer for the old woman. She placed some money in Blue's outstretched hand, and they've been friends ever since. Sort of.

That afternoon, Blue shared a piece of her past with Fiamma. She explained that she ended up in the wheelchair while chasing the love of her life, a man who was leaving on one of the many trains that took him away from her. After hearing the story, Fiamma couldn't help but think Blue had been a bit foolish to chase someone who was running away from her. At that moment, Blue glared at her, as if she'd read her mind. She stared Fiamma straight in the eye and hissed, "So, you think you're smarter, stronger, just 'cause you're young and still walk tall, huh? Think you'll never chase someone who means more than it all, huh? You've no idea... how little it takes... how thin the line between your fate and mine. One slip, one lie, a string of wrongs, and watch the stars misalign. Joy turns bitter, love to ache... and everything you held just breaks. You're no different from the rest who pass me by, with lowered gaze or a judging eye. You think the gap's so wide between us two, but you're wrong. You're wrong... and deep down, you know it too."

Fiamma fell silent. She was stunned and a bit offended, and for a moment, she wanted to leave. She wanted to get as far away as possible from this crazy woman, her strange way of speaking, and the wheelchair parked by the wall of an abandoned shop. But she stayed, curious to hear the rest of the story.

She sat on the filthy step in front of the abandoned shop and watched the wisps of smoke that escaped Blue's mouth as she traced her memories.

Blue is a chain smoker. Fiamma, like many others, brings her cigarettes whenever she visits. Blue hardly ever reacts to those gifts. Sometimes, she just lifts her chin to the sky, as if to say, "You did the right thing."

Blue can be rude at times, but there's something reassuring about her. Under that funny blue hat, there's a sort of civility. She's one of those thick-skinned people who you just know is good deep down, one of those people who became that way out of necessity. Fiamma enjoys her time with Blue because there's no pressure to talk. Sometimes, after handing over her daily offerings, a beer, some wine, money, a sandwich, she just sits quietly. Blue knows Fiamma doesn't want to talk, and she sits there too, as if it's the most normal thing in the world. Sometimes, they spend whole afternoons in silence: Fiamma studying, Blue reading, smoking, sipping wine or beer, just staring into the distance.

At other times, Blue shares pearls of wisdom that leave Fiamma speechless. It's almost as if, beneath that blue hat, she has a crystal ball or a third eye that sees everything and only speaks when she chooses. Almost absentmindedly.

Once, after a couple of beers, Blue started talking about poetry. She told Fiamma that she loved reading poetry when she was young: Shakespeare, Lord Byron, Dylan Thomas. She still remembered some poems by heart.

"You know, those verses saved me from oblivion. If it weren't for poetry, I'd be in real trouble…" she confessed, looking around. "Reading's the thread that's kept me alive, in this mess of a world where I barely survive. Look around: this isn't life, it's a fight. Only the words keep my soul alight."

Blue seemed far away when she said this, though she was looking directly at Fiamma. Her eyes were distant, staring through Fiamma, beyond her. Fiamma didn't interrupt, just let her speak.

"The truth is, you have to find poetry in the unpoetic… in the artificial rustling of plastic branches, for example…"

Blue pointed to a fake plant near the café's entrance. "You have to find the poetry in the corners of your mind, imagine it against the grey bars of metal lights, feel its honeyed notes as it runs along the cold asphalt, long for it as it hides, unsure, in the nooks of what's possible… then gather it up, embrace it, keep it warm…"

Fiamma thought of the pile of trash she saw burning outside her window a few nights ago. It lit up the night, sending bursts of color above the trash can.

"You see, love can be taken from us in an instant, at any moment. But poetry is forever, forever, and for anyone." She took another drag on her cigarette, almost to the filter, as if trying to inhale it all. Every word came out in a ring of smoke. Fiamma silently watched her and the smoke rings.

"Poetry comes like those flowers that grow in the strangest places, unasked for, seemingly unnecessary: between train tracks where trains hardly stop, far from crowded stations… growing, wilting, and growing again, without water, without sun. Poetry grows. And that's it. It asks nothing of us."

Blue rarely looks at Fiamma when she speaks. She mostly stares ahead or glances distractedly at the bar door she'll never enter, at the outdoor tables she'll never sit at, at the neon lights that hypnotize her.

Blue talks, and Fiamma listens. She speaks, and Fiamma understands that Blue always has something new to say, even if it's unsolicited. It's almost like Blue can see deep into Fiamma, understanding the anger behind her made-up eyes, the sadness hiding beneath her fake indifference.

Today, for the first time, Fiamma ends up asking her a direct question. She asks Blue how it is possible to live when you have uncontrollable hate and anger inside you, feelings that hold you back. Fiamma's anger is blind, scentless, and speechless, and she's carried it inside for as long as she can remember. It influences every moment of every day. She asks without thinking of Blue's situation, her wheelchair and how she ended up there, without wondering if Blue's anger is more justified than hers, or how Blue might judge her. She blurts out the question, hoping for an answer that might help.

And Blue, as expected, responds.

"What matters, I think, is not turning to rage, not letting your fury become your cage. You've got to be more than the ache in your chest, more than the numbness that never finds rest. Let your pain be fire, not a flame that consumes, let your grief hold a lantern that pierces the gloom. Joy that ignites when hearts intertwine, and fury that burns without crossing the line. What matters is this: to be wholly you, free in the storm, fierce and true. Alive in the fight, no fear of the fall, chasing the joys that seem too tall. Imperfect and perfect, in heat and in stone, a warrior rising, even alone. Hold on to that space deep under your skin, where you toast to the night with a moon-slice grin. Even when no one sees you there, what matters is that you're still aware."

Fiamma isn't sure whether she's heard these words before or if Blue is speaking to her or just mumbling to herself. She doesn't know if Blue understands her anger or if her words are the ramblings of a warped mind. But somehow, in that moment, those words make sense to Fiamma. They give her a tiny bit of hope, a thread to hold onto. In silence, Fiamma stands up from the dirty step, thanks her friend, and walks away, feeling just a little bit better. Blue doesn't answer, doesn't even look at her. She takes another drag of her cigarette, eyes fixed on the door of the café, on the nameless people who pass in and out, on the neon lights that are always on, day and night, even in the sun. As Fiamma heads down the stairs to the underground, she hears Blue's voice one last time: "You have too bright a future ahead of you to live in the anger of the past!"

The rest of the words are lost in the clatter of feet, clanging metal, and rumbling trains.

BLUE

I've forgotten my name, it's faded, gone.

Don't recall when I last spoke it aloud, if ever at all. Fiamma calls me Blue, and that name clings tight. Blue like my hat. Blue like this night. This endless night I've worn for years, in a chair that cradles pain and fears. Watching people come and go by the track, where my journey was meant to begin, but never came back. Since that day, no one's asked who I am, or why I'm rooted here like some silent dam. This cradle of nothing, it's where I remain, in a world where staying still means bearing the strain. Fiamma... she's a spark in the pitch. A flicker, a flame, a flame that won't quit.

There's something I recall even less than my name: the night this all started, the darkness, the shame. I remember the station, dressed in different attire, and the train with its teeth, its screech, its fire. I remember the poison rushing my veins, the metallic scream, the echo of pain. And in my mind, there's a place where words rot: letters unsent, confessions forgot. And his face, too young, too dear, brings guilt to my lips and draws out a tear. His face still lingers, soft and warm, the one piece of me untouched by the storm. This station, it's become my world entire, where time runs fast but my limbs tire. And yet... something in me still dares to dream, still aches to run, still wants to scream. To chase him again, with wind at my feet, with legs full of hope and a heart that beats.

That girl from the past? She's not gone, not quite. She still burns, still loves, still sees the light. She'd laugh at this woman, all brittle and grey, waiting for death to carry her away.

LIGHT

I did it again a few hours ago. Opened the fridge, then the pantry, then back to the fridge, and again to the pantry. My hands to my mouth over and over, without stopping, except for a quick sip of water to swallow the thick paste, the empty mash I'd just chewed, mixed and drenched in saliva. My tongue feels paralyzed, unable to sense any taste at all. Cold, hot, salty, sweet: it all blends into one flavorless mess. A massive gulp of nothing.

I always watch myself from the outside when this happens, like people who say they've had near-death experiences. I see myself staring at the food I still have to choke down. I see myself with vacant eyes, thinking about how much more I could possibly eat. But I never look at the bites that are about to enter my mouth. They slide into me almost unnoticed. They invade my body, without my consent. It's a rape of food, unwanted and endless, without pleasure, without release, without a single shudder or climax.

I was about to head to the bathroom afterward. But then, I don't know what hit me… I needed to lie down for just a minute. I placed my hand on my stomach and felt the movements inside: fast, steady, almost rhythmic jerks, repeating, like signals from deep within. I wondered if that's how pregnant women feel when the baby kicks inside their belly. I kept watching my swollen stomach, my hand resting on it, imagining there was life moving inside me. I forgot to go to the bathroom, and instead drifted into the sweetest sleep. I dreamed of a cradle, surrounded by a ring of bees or maybe butterflies, colorful and joyful. It was like the cradle I had as a child. A noisy, musical cradle, with insects dancing in circles, chasing each other, aimless, with no direction.

Ring a-ring o' roses, a pocket full of posies, a-tishoo! a-tishoo! We all fall down… Round and round, spinning and spinning, everything but the cradle where the child sleeps with dreams untainted. Dreams without vomit, without all the other shit.

Now, as I write, I can't help but think how nice it would be to keep pretending, just for another nine months. Nine months away from this sickness that's dragging me toward my death, pretending that life is still moving, still fighting inside me.

She felt like taking a long walk, just wandering around on her own, avoiding the bus or subway. She wanted to step out and go wherever the music blaring in her earbuds would take her. Her apartment is three miles from the center of Rome, with half the route paved and the other half covered in cobblestones and trash. Over three miles of dirt and grime. Yet Fiamma walks the whole way without even the slightest hint of fatigue. She takes paths and strolls through hidden alleys, places where the walls are covered in graffiti with stories more compelling than history itself, spots where shop doors are shut tight, plastered with spray paint and defeat. The anger of those who dreamed of a different life, a bigger bank account, or simply a better love, a quieter corner of happiness to curl up in. As she walks, Fiamma imagines the millions of stories behind the graffiti on homes and ancient buildings. The quiet desperation locked away behind doors sealed by bankruptcy. The silence amidst the chaos of cars zooming by, oblivious to it all. Insensitive to the emptiness around her.

Walking through Rome today means admiring the colossal monuments, even if you've seen them hundreds of times before, and turning a blind eye to the discarded mattresses under the pine trees, or the human figures hidden beneath sheets of newspaper. Fiamma has been walking slowly for hours, never once checking the watch she wears like a leather cuff, the face and hands that bind her to the passing of time. She's covered stretches of road, unraveling beneath her feet like an invisible carpet, without making a sound.

By the time she reaches the Church of Santa Maria della Vittoria, she has no idea what time it is. All she knows, and she's not sure how she knows it, maybe it's just intuition or a sixth sense, is that he will be exactly where she hopes he'll be. He's like a mental image that's come to life. It's as if they have an unspoken meeting, planned and confirmed long ago.

And *he* – her dreamt-up love, invented to make her mother happy – is still there, in the exact spot she left him, as if frozen in time, waiting, as if bound by a silent agreement. He's sitting on one of the steps of the church, but there's no stool this time, no bottles, no crowd. He's ditched his artist's robes for regular clothes, now blending in as someone who casually watches life pass by. Fiamma watches him from a distance for a moment. He doesn't seem to be waiting for anyone. In fact, he looks like someone who has nothing and no one to wait for, nothing to do in the world right now. His right elbow rests on his leg, his head leans on his open palm, as if his thoughts are too heavy to bear. His left hand hangs limply between his legs, and his fingers move up and down, practicing an imaginary scale. Fiamma can't tell what he's looking at, or if his eyes are even open. She decides to find out and slowly walks toward him, looking directly at him, head slightly tilted. She wears the smile of someone who's just bumped into a long-lost friend and is about to greet him.

"Hey, hi!" he says with a smile, anticipating Fiamma's greeting. He lifts his head, and Fiamma finally sees the color of his eyes. They're amber, just as she imagined when she first saw him, golden with copper tinges near the pupils. Her grandmother would have said they were wolf eyes, eyes to run from, fierce and untamed.

"I remember you!" he says after a brief pause. "I noticed you in the crowd the other day when I was playing. Did you like the show?"

Fiamma replays the scene in her mind: the boy, the bottles, the mallets, his eyes, and the music.

"Hi… Well, yes, it was amazing," she replies, after an awkward silence. "You're really talented… Have you been doing it for long?"

He smiles sheepishly, gazing off into the distance as if he has to think about it.

"No, I haven't been playing music on bottles for too long," he says finally, a smile tugging at his lips, "but I used to play it on water glasses not too long ago."

"What… what do you mean? Are you kidding?" Fiamma asks skeptically.

"No, no, I'm not kidding. I really did play music on water glasses," he responds, a bit defensive. "The process is a little different. No mallets. You use your fingers, which you wet in a bowl. The glasses need to have different amounts of water, and you rub your fingers along the edges. The key is the movement… Sorry, it's harder to explain than to do, really. Maybe I can show you sometime. The problem with glasses is I'm kind of clumsy and end up breaking them when I move them. It's expensive. But bottles are tougher. And you can find them anywhere, sometimes even in the trash." He lowers his voice on that last part, glancing away like he's embarrassed. Fiamma doesn't react as though she hasn't heard him, or that she doesn't care if she did.

"Yeah. So I guess you travel a lot… Oh, sorry, what did you say your name was?"

"Lorenzo… My name's Lorenzo. Yeah, you could say I travel a lot. It's been a year now. I don't stay in one place for more than a couple of months. I've traveled all over Italy, and next month I'm making the big move: I'm taking the ferry from Civitavecchia to Barcelona. I've always wanted to go there since I was a kid. I've never been, even though my mom was born there."

"Where do you usually sleep?" Fiamma's fascination with this total stranger drives her to ask.

"On the street!" Lorenzo jokes, laughing. "Well, I might end up there one day, but for now, I'm *couchsurfing*. There's always someone willing to let me crash for the night. It's all free, of course. In exchange for hospitality, I cook, clean… and play my music, of course."

"Wow. That sounds amazing. You must meet all sorts of different people… But aren't you ever scared? Staying with strangers? I mean, there are some pretty weird people out there…"

Lorenzo cuts her off almost immediately. "There are far fewer weirdos out there than you think, trust me. When I travel, I meet the nicest people. I've never had any trouble with anyone."

Then he suddenly turns serious. His eyes darken, as if a shadow has fallen over them. "To be honest, I've felt safer in other people's homes than in my own…" he says, pausing for a long moment. Fiamma is taken aback. She's tempted to ask him to explain, but he cuts off her curiosity.

"But that's a whole other story, and I don't think I want to share it now" he finishes, almost reading her mind.

"So, out of everyone you've met in Italy, who's the one you liked the most?" Fiamma asks to break the silence that's fallen between them.

Lorenzo answers without hesitation, "Yorgos," he says, smiling. "He's a Greek guy I met in Umbria, in Perugia. He works and studies there. He made me feel at home right away. After five minutes, it felt like we'd known each other forever. We write to each other a lot. He calls me 'Italian brother,' and I call him 'Greek brother'. Sooner or later, I'll have to go back to Perugia to visit him. Or maybe to Crete, his home, once he finishes university. The guy I'm staying with now is totally different. He's nice and all, even gave me keys to his place. He said I can stay as long as I want, come and go whenever, but… I don't know. There's no real connection. You see… For me, couchsurfing isn't just about finding a place to sleep so I can travel on a budget. It's about meeting people, making friends, and touching other people's lives."

"And who is this new guy? What's his name?"

"Roberto… He's the guy I'm staying with now."

"Right… And this Roberto guy is a bit distant, huh?"

"Exactly. Maybe he's just shy or something. I don't know. But it's like having a landlord, a total stranger. Don't get me wrong, he's nice. I feel bad talking like this about him…"

"You're not saying anything bad. You're just saying you wish he was a bit more open, more engaging with you. You're not criticizing him or anything."

Lorenzo smiles sweetly and nods. Fiamma feels her knees weaken. She feels utterly helpless when he smiles. She tries to mask her emotions and adopts a serious expression. She asks Lorenzo if it's true that he's never been afraid to meet someone with bad intentions. "I can't believe it doesn't scare you to stay in the homes of strangers, people you've never met before. I mean, what if one of them is… not a serial killer, but just someone looking to take your money…"

Lorenzo bursts out laughing. "Optimistic of you! What could they possibly take from me? My backpack's junk?

The most valuable thing I own is *Red Fox*, my motorcycle. But I doubt anyone would want it. It flies like the wind, but only when I'm riding it because I know how to handle it… and, most of all, I know how to fix it when it breaks down!"

Fiamma now feels embarrassed, as though she just said something totally foolish. She shifts uncomfortably on the cold step, which now seems even colder. She looks away, hoping to find something intelligent to say to redeem herself. Lorenzo seems to sense this and tries to help: "I was just kidding… I totally get what you mean. If I were a girl, I'd have a lot more to worry about. Couchsurfing can be risky, I guess, because it relies on trust and the reviews people leave on the website. But let me tell you this: for every handful of nutcases, there are thousands and thousands of normal people. And hundreds of people worth meeting. I'm not just talking about the hosts, but everyone you meet while traveling. I mean… if Roberto hadn't hosted me, I probably wouldn't have met you…"

Fiamma feels her face flush, smiles at Lorenzo, then looks down. The pavement suddenly seems incredibly interesting, and her gaze is locked on it.

"One of my favorite sayings is: Opportunity never knocks twice at anyone's door," Lorenzo continues. "If you get a chance to do something fun and you miss it, whether out of fear or some other reason, you'll probably regret it."

Fiamma finally raises her eyes from the pavement. "I think you're right…" she says. "But… call me a pessimist, I'm more inclined to think the world has a handful of normal people and thousands and thousands of nutcases…"

Lorenzo starts laughing, raises his hands to his head,

and shakes it dramatically. "Alright, alright, sweet damsel in pessimistic distress. I guess my mission in this sad world is to prove you wrong. I'll change your mind. You'll see. You'll start trusting people…"

"The damsel in pessimistic distress is called Fiamma… and she dares you to change her mind."

"Okay… right, Fiamma… let's start now. How about we meet next Saturday? I could pick you up at your place. No, wait… since you don't trust people, let's meet at a café or somewhere public near your place. That way you don't have to give some stranger your address."

Lorenzo pauses, grins at Fiamma, and adds, "And, of course, I'd love to have your phone number… I'll take you to the fair if you want. It's been a while since I've been, and I'd love to go with you."

*

She felt an immediate need to share the news with Elife. After all, Elife is her best friend, and she wanted to fill her in on this small, but lovely change in her life. With all the mess she's been dealing with over the years, and her looming final exams – alongside all her fears and insecurities – this thing with Lorenzo, while small, is something really beautiful.

They agreed to meet in the park halfway between their places. It's usually a lovely spot, full of lush greenery and ancient trees, a calm and inviting space. Usually, but not today. It's a gray day, and the rain has started, leaving Fiamma completely unprepared. She's dressed too lightly for the weather, with no jacket and definitely no umbrella.

Thankfully, Elife is always punctual and, unlike her friend, always prepared. She brought an umbrella big enough for both.

"If it weren't for you, Eli..." Fiamma sighs, huddling under the umbrella. She's soaked through and already bracing herself for the aspirin she'll need later. "Just what I needed today, the rain! Look at me, I'm drenched... I feel like I've got algae growing on my socks!"

Elife just looks at her and shakes her head, giving a mock reprimand: "Didn't you check the weather forecast? Clearly not... otherwise, you'd have brought an umbrella like I did. There was an 88% chance of rain. 88%! Who goes outside without an umbrella when there's that high a chance of rain? And it's still March! The month might be winding down, but it's not over yet. Remember what they say about March, that it's a trickster, always changing its mind? If you're not into weather reports, at least follow some commonsense wisdom. Honestly, Fiamma..."

"Okay, okay, Eli! I get it!" Fiamma huffs, rolling her eyes. "I should've checked the forecast, or looked at the sky before I left. I should've been smarter... Alright! I made a mistake. The rain's already getting me down, don't add to it."

"That's another thing I don't get. Why do you hate the rain so much? I mean, I don't mind it. Sure, too much could give you a nasty cold, or worse, bronchitis or pneumonia. But you've barely gotten wet! You got a few drops, that's it. In fact, I read somewhere that the ancient Romans believed rainwater was a miracle beauty tonic. Even in more recent times, people used it for homemade face tonics. Although, these days, I guess I wouldn't use it since it's pretty polluted. Did you know it contains aluminum and barium? They say that..."

"Eli, stop!" Fiamma interrupts, clearly frustrated. "I'm not planning on turning the rain into a skincare routine, okay? Honestly, the only thing I like about rain is the smell it leaves behind on the earth and the grass after a downpour. That unique smell that fills the air afterward. That's the only thing I care about when it rains. Period."

"Oh, I know what you mean!" Elife says. "That earthy, sharp smell, right? It's called *petrichor*. I was just reading about it the other day. Apparently, it's caused by tiny water droplets and airborne bacteria interacting with the ground..."

"Great!" Fiamma cuts her off again before she can dive into yet another long-winded science rant. "Just what I needed, more science! This is just like when you told me that comets apparently smell like manure and rotten eggs. And now you've ruined one of the only poetic things left on Earth by turning it into... some science lesson about bacteria. Can I just tell you something nice that happened to me yesterday?"

"Okay, go ahead," Elife says, still looking disappointed that she didn't get to finish her scientific tidbit. She knows all about petrichor and would've loved to share it with Fiamma.

"Remember that guy we saw the other day when we went out for my birthday? The one playing bottles? Well..." Fiamma takes a deep breath, gathering all her excitement to tell Elife the full story. She tells her about the way her heart skipped a beat when she saw him, their conversation, the strange color of his eyes, his couch-surfing lifestyle, and the invitation to the funfair.

Elife listens quietly, but Fiamma can tell something's off. Her friend looks uncomfortable, avoiding her gaze and shifting from foot to foot, like she's about to leave.

"Eli... what's going on?"

"I don't know, Fiamma... you tell me. Everything's fine, right?" Elife says after a long pause. "I mean, have you heard yourself? You're about to meet a total stranger. A street performer, no less. A guy who lives day-to-day, and you barely know him. It's dangerous, don't you get that? What's wrong with you?"

"Whoa, hold on!" Fiamma stares at her in disbelief. Her expression is a mix of shock and disappointment. "Eli, I get that we're different. You're all about being practical and careful, while I'm just a normal teen who sometimes does dumb stuff. But this? This is too much, don't you think? I was hoping you'd be happy for me, or at least indifferent. But this reaction? It's over the top. It's not like I told you I went to his place and slept with him the minute I saw him. All he knows about me is my name and my phone number. We're meeting in public, at a funfair, on a Saturday afternoon. Surrounded by tons of people. Sure, he could be a psycho, or even a serial killer, I guess, and anything could happen, but the odds of that happening are tiny. And bad things can happen anywhere. Even in your own home, the place you're supposed to be the safest. You know that, right?" She clenches her fist so tight it starts to shake. She barely notices the gesture, but she feels the tightness in her chest. "And damn it, I'm still young! Even if I were doing the dumbest thing ever, I have the right to do it!"

Elife doesn't say anything, just stares off into the distance.

"Alright... alright, Fiamma," Elife finally murmurs. "You're right. Do whatever you want..." Then she moves the umbrella slightly closer to Fiamma, almost as if she's trying to shield her from something beyond the rain.

If it weren't for the rain and the wind, Fiamma might've noticed the tiny tears that had appeared in Elife's eyes.

Lorenzo is right on time, or he's been waiting for a while. He's sitting on his shiny red motorcycle at the café near Fiamma's house.

"I'd like you to meet *Red Fox*!" he says with pride as soon as he spots her, pointing to the bike.

"Red Fox…" Fiamma repeats slowly, with a hint of sarcasm. "Where'd you come up with that name?"

"Well, the color's pretty obvious, right? But you're probably more interested in why I picked that animal. Wolves and lions are too cliché. Everyone loves them. So, I thought a fox would be a better choice. They're beautiful and super adaptable, kind of like this bike." Lorenzo pats the back of the motorcycle as he talks, almost like a jockey talking to his horse.

"My Red Fox has been through a lot of different environments, too. And, as you probably know, foxes are solitary hunters. They're more active at night than during the day. Same for me, I'm out mostly at night. During the day, I'm busy working my gigs."

"Alright, alright, I'm sold!" Fiamma interrupts, quickly slipping on the spare helmet. "Let's see if Red Fox is as fast as it looks!"

When they get to the amusement park, Fiamma feels a pang in her chest. The last time she was at one was with her dad. She can't remember much, she was probably four or five, but what sticks out is how everything seemed so huge, and the ride she wanted to go on most was out of reach. "No way, not the rollercoaster!" her dad had said firmly. "Of all the rides, why that one? There are tons of other fun rides here... you're too little for the rollercoaster..."

Fiamma remembers his words perfectly. They still echo in her head like defeat. Everything else about that day has faded, the bright colors of her childhood are now a dull grey, swallowed up by the dampness of the day, which seems to absorb all the color around it. The joyful sounds and voices that once made her smile are now distant and warped. Even the smell of cotton candy is gone. But her dad's words, the ones that kept her from the rollercoaster, are as clear as ever. So, when Lorenzo asks what ride she wants to go on first, she doesn't hesitate.

"Let's do the rollercoaster. I've never been on one. I've seen videos and I know I'll love it... the fear, the excitement, the adrenaline... feeling your heart drop when you suddenly plunge down and the ground disappears beneath you... yes, let's start there."

"The rollercoaster's not my favorite ride, but if that's what you want, we'll do it, ma'am" Lorenzo says, locking up his motorcycle.

"I usually like the funhouse mirrors. The way the images get all warped reminds me of childhood memories, distant and changed. But rollercoasters are more exciting, so let's go!"

*

"So, what can I tell you about the amusement parks that you don't already know?" Lorenzo furrows his brow, making a silly face as he looks up at the sky, almost like he's hoping for some inspiration. Fiamma can't help but laugh.

"Hey, this is serious! I'm trying to remember some fun facts I've read about amusement parks, so I can impress you with my vast knowledge on the subject" he says dramatically.

His expression and tone are anything but serious, but Fiamma decides to humor him.

"Let me think…Aha, got it!" he says after a brief pause. "Okay, I don't really have any cool fun facts about amusement parks at the moment, but I do know some stuff about rollercoasters, since you're so into them. So, do you know why rollercoasters are called *Montagne Russe*, in Italy? It's because they were invented in Russia! But here's the funny part, Russians call them 'American Mountains.' I guess they have a hard time taking credit for their own inventions. In Italy, we also call them 'Ottovolante,' because a German guy named Otto brought the first ones to Italy." Lorenzo takes a quick glance at Fiamma before continuing, "Oh, and did you know that in about ten years, all rollercoasters will be floating in the air? Some British scientists have developed a system that defies gravity. Essentially, we'll still be doing all the same moves as today, including the loop-de-loop, but without any tracks. No need to worry about Marty McFly's hoverboard anymore!"

"Are you serious?" Fiamma asks, wide-eyed.

"Well, I kinda made that last part up…" Lorenzo admits. "You didn't seem that interested, so I had to say something exciting. But hey, it could totally happen! The important thing is that the fun-fact you reacted to the most was the one I just made up on the spot! My imagination is way more interesting than reality!"

"Yeah, right!" Fiamma says, giving him a look that's a mix of disapproval and amusement. "But seriously, you don't have to try to impress me all the time. I'm not one of your audience members that you need to wow with your tricks. Come on, let's just get our tickets."

*

After the third rollercoaster ride, Lorenzo is completely wiped out, while Fiamma seems to get more energized with every twist and turn. It's like each speed burst is giving her more energy.

"Listen!" Lorenzo shouts, trying to be heard over the others on the ride and his own screams, which he's been holding back just to keep his cool in front of Fiamma. "You know the guy I'm staying with, Roberto? He's a designer and travels a lot. The day after tomorrow, he's leaving for a fashion show in Tuscany and won't be back until Wednesday. He told me I could invite someone over, if I want."

Another twist, another stomach lurch for Lorenzo. He's starting to get a slight headache, but he doesn't want to complain. "So anyway..." he continues, shouting over the screams but barely audible, "...he's a bit of a loner, but he's super nice and generous. So, before you say no, think about that old saying: 'Opportunity doesn't knock twice.' And there's also 'Carpe Diem' and stuff... So, if you want, I can give you the address, and you can come over to my borrowed place for dinner. We'll have sushiiii..."

The last word echoes loudly in the air as they zoom around yet another loop. Fiamma laughs out loud, partly from shock, partly from embarrassment, and partly because she finally realizes that Lorenzo's had enough and is totally worn out from the ride.

"I don't know what's more surprising, the invite or the sushi," she says, still trying to mask her laughter.

"Wait, what? You don't like sushi? Please tell me you're not one of those people who refuses to eat raw fish…"

"No…well, I don't really know. I've never tried it. It's just that…it's not exactly the kind of food I'd expect on a date…" Fiamma's face turns red the second she says the word *date*. Suddenly, she doesn't feel like laughing anymore. Date? Such a weird, old-fashioned word. And besides, who says this is a date? Maybe he just wants to hang out with a bunch of sushi-loving friends at his place, with a bunch of beautiful girls dressed as geishas.

Lorenzo's grin only makes Fiamma feel more awkward. He's just staring at her, with that satisfied look on his face, and she has no idea how to take it.

When the ride finally slows down and comes to a stop, Fiamma feels lost. The sense of danger and weightlessness that kept her grounded are now gone.

"I swear, you'll love my sushi. And after you try it, you won't want to eat anything else on a *date*…" He emphasizes the last word, drawing it out with a smile as he watches Fiamma turn even more red, avoiding his gaze.

"And I'll tell you a few cool facts about Japanese culture while you're there. Trust me, it's gonna be great. So, you're in, right?"

I'm not sure I'm strong enough to bear happiness.

It takes more energy to pursue happiness than it does to give in to anger and sadness. Happiness doesn't come easily: it must be held tightly, cradled in your arms, and carefully guided through the daily minefields of life. You have to steer it gently, just as you would a child, holding its hand as you lead it past pain, bad memories, and the scars left by sorrow. To carry it without letting it slip away requires strength, and you need strong arms to keep it from falling, all the way to the end of your journey. Anger and sadness, on the other hand, are easier to manage. They take the lead, showing you the way. You don't need to do anything, just let them take over.

There are times when I feel so happy that I can hardly stand it.

It happens when I hear music that touches me deeply, or when I read a poem that resonates, or when I watch a film that moves me. It's strange and hard to explain, but in those moments, I close my eyes, almost to capture that feeling or block out everything else. Sometimes I curl up with my knees to my chest, and other times I pace back and forth or even skip around the room. There are times when I feel like I could scream, and I'm grateful for the walls around me, protecting me from the outside world.

It's strange, almost absurd, and I can't quite understand it myself, but sometimes, I feel so overwhelmed by happiness that it almost makes me want to die. Not because I want to end my life, but because I can't handle all of it, or maybe because I'm not ready for it.

Yes, that's it, I feel so happy, it makes me want to die.

Today was one of those days. I was listening to Comptine d'un autre été: L'après-midi *by Yann Tiersen, from the* Amélie *soundtrack, a film I love. I found it on YouTube, paired with a video full of poetic imagery. The music and images still swirl inside me, here in the silence of my small apartment, which feels like my little shell. I try to piece it all together, like a puzzle of emotions that has no clear beginning or end, constantly shifting, blending, and pulling away.*

It takes so much energy to handle happiness. And if you're someone who's known real joy only to lose it in the worst way, the struggle is even greater. Fear can pin you down, freeze your body, block your voice, and all that's left are your eyes, wide open, forced to watch as happiness passes you by, and you can do nothing to stop it or even get its attention.

Roberto's house is sleek and modern. As soon as Fiamma steps inside, she's greeted by a large open-concept living space with an island kitchen. Instead of a traditional dining table, there's a counter that runs parallel to the kitchen area like an extension. In front of it, six American-style bar stools stand lined up in perfect order, like soldiers at attention. Lorenzo gestures to one of them, inviting her to sit.

"The show is about to begin. Get comfortable!"

Fiamma sits on the stool at the far left, feeling a bit uneasy.

"So… I'm guessing you know what sushi is, right?" Lorenzo asks, twirling a pair of wooden chopsticks in the air.

"Sort of… I've heard of it, obviously. I know what it looks like from movies. But like I told you the other day, I've never actually tried it."

"Great! Consider this an initiation! After you've had sushi, you'll fall in love with it and never be able to live without it!"

Fiamma feels more nervous than curious or excited about trying something completely new, but she doesn't want to kill Lorenzo's excitement, so she gives him a reassuring smile.

"Well, I won't bore you with the history of sushi or the details on how to prepare the rice, which is a bit lengthy. I'll just say that it's made with white, sweet, short-grain rice. First, you wash it until the water runs clear, and then steam it. There are a few extra steps, but I'll skip those and jump straight to making one of the most popular kinds of sushi: *maki*, the classic rice roll wrapped in nori seaweed, with fish or vegetables inside."

As Lorenzo speaks, he moves with ease, almost like a pro chef in his own kitchen.

He unrolls a bamboo mat, placing a thin, dry, dark green sheet of nori on top.

"First, you place the nori on this handy bamboo mat, called a makisu. Then, after moistening your hands with water, you spread a layer of rice, leaving one end uncovered. Wet hands are key to prevent the rice from sticking, of course. Got it so far?"

Fiamma nods, eager to see the next steps.

"Perfect! Now, once the rice is spread, it's time to add the fish. I've already sliced the fish to speed things up, so now I just place a strip of it in the center of the rice. Then, I wet the uncovered edge of the nori, lift the bamboo mat, and roll everything up tightly. You have to do it slowly but firmly."

"Cool!" Fiamma smiles, finally lifting her gaze from the mesmerizing motion of Lorenzo's hands. "What's next?"

"Now the maki are almost done! All we need to do is slice the roll into pieces, about one to two centimeters thick. Go ahead and give it a try. Meanwhile, I'll get the nigiri ready. You know, those little rice dumplings topped with fish? You've probably seen them in Japanese cartoons. They look easy, but there's actually a bit of technique involved... Just watch and learn from your personal chef, *Lorenzo-sensei*."

"All right, *Lorenzo-sensei! Fiamma-san* is here to learn!" Fiamma says with exaggerated enthusiasm, carefully slicing the sushi rolls. "But tell me, where did this love for sushi come from?"

"To be honest, I like everything about sushi. I love both the fish and the rice, so together it's a winning combo. Plus, I love how colorful and fun they are… they just give off happy vibes. And I love how you eat it right after it's made, in one bite, without chewing it or anything. It makes me think of life: you just take it in, all at once. Anyway, sushi aside, I really like Japanese culture in general. It's fascinating! Ever heard of Kintsugi?"

"Honestly, no," Fiamma admits, a bit embarrassed. "Never heard of it."

"It's one of the many things that drew me to Japan. Kintsugi is a technique where you repair broken items using liquid gold or silver. So, when something like pottery breaks, instead of throwing it away or replacing it, they repair it and fill the cracks with gold. The crack becomes a part of the piece, and it's treated like a precious addition. Isn't that amazing? But what really fascinates me is the philosophy behind it. The idea that when something, or someone, gets broken…hurt in some way… it can actually become more beautiful. Isn't that extraordinary?" Lorenzo's face lights up as he talks, eager to share his excitement.

Fiamma smiles, thinking back to her childhood and the disastrous crafts she had to do in school. "For someone who's always hated glue and anything sticky, that's definitely amazing." She becomes serious again. "Using precious metal instead of clear adhesive… I have to admit, that's really fascinating."

"It's not just about using one material over another," Lorenzo corrects her. "I think Kintsugi really highlights the difference between trying to hide a crack and celebrating it. You see, when we use glue, we try to put the pieces together in a way that hides the break. Kintsugi does the opposite: it makes the crack the focal point. To me, that says something important: a crack… a scar, in a person's case… shouldn't be something to be ashamed of. It should be something to highlight. Anything broken and repaired has its own unique beauty, just like pottery that's been fixed with gold. Each piece ends up with a different, one-of-a-kind design, a unique pattern that can never be replicated. Think about it… don't you think that's just beautiful?"

Fiamma pauses for a moment, looking at him with a soft smile. "I've thought about it already… really thought about it…" she says, widening her smile to show nearly all her teeth. "And I think it's truly amazing. From now on, I'll look at my scars differently. I'll respect the Japanese even more. And I'll proudly wear my golden scars."

*

"I'm sure someone's already told you this, but you have a beautiful name," Lorenzo says, avoiding eye contact as he focuses on the salmon maki he's just picked up with his chopsticks.

"Thank you… yeah, a lot of people have said that, but it's always nice to hear," Fiamma responds, smiling as she watches Lorenzo, trying to mimic his technique. "My dad chose it for me…" she continues, struggling to grab the tuna nigiri, which keeps slipping off her chopsticks. "He's the one who picked it. My mom had no say in it at all. Not that she cared much about what I was called. The only thing she ever really did for me was carry me for nine months. That's it. I'm sure my dad was the only one who ever touched her belly. My mom probably just spent the whole time stressing about how much weight she'd gained, looking like a balloon with legs. Honestly, I think she saw me as a burden for the entire 40 weeks I was inside her. Like a bump, but on the wrong side. I imagine she felt like that the whole time…"

Lorenzo interrupts, sounding upset. "Why are you so hard on your mom? How do you even know she felt that way during her pregnancy? I think you're being pretty harsh. How can you be so sure?"

"I just am."

Her blunt tone and intense gaze silence Lorenzo. She pushes the chopsticks aside, frustrated with trying to eat like a typical Japanese person, and picks up the nigiri with her fingers. "My mom's always been way too obsessed with herself to care about anyone else. She's obsessed with her looks… I really doubt she was thrilled about getting as big as a whale when she was pregnant with me. She loses it over even gaining a pound. We've never talked about it, but I'm sure I was an unplanned pregnancy… one of those mistakes people talk about."

"Well… if that's how you feel," Lorenzo mutters, unconvinced, but deciding to let it go for now.

"Why did your dad choose to name you Fiamma? It's a beautiful name, but not exactly common…"

"He had a reason for it: my dad was a fire-eater." Fiamma speaks with her mouth full, enjoying the tuna and rice as they melt in her mouth. "He's been fascinated by fire since he was a kid. I used to watch him perform in the streets of Rome when I was little. Sometimes he'd go to other towns too. He loved traveling. My parents lived like gypsies before I was born. They had a caravan and moved from place to place. As far as I know, they were happy. And the three of us were happy, until my dad got sick. But that's how I remember it. Who knows… maybe it was just him and me who were happy, and my mom was lost in thoughts of the life she could've had if she hadn't had us. Or maybe I was the only happy one in the family, the innocent kind of happiness that only kids can have."

"What happened to him exactly? You talk about him like he's gone, so... I'm guessing..."

"You're right. My dad passed away. He had stomach cancer. Once he got sick, he stopped performing. His doctors, my mom, and my grandmother made him stop completely. He couldn't keep moving from place to place, especially because he didn't have the strength anymore. You know what? I think that's when my dad really started to fade. In just days, he went from being this strong, energetic guy to someone who looked like a shadow of himself. I think his illness got worse because he couldn't do what he loved anymore."

"Sometimes I wonder how things would've turned out if he hadn't gotten sick," Fiamma says softly. "I think about the years Death took away from me, the trips we could've still gone on, the life I could've been living if he were still here with me. Maybe he would've taught me some art, and I'd be a street performer too."

"I'm sorry for your loss..." Lorenzo's voice is barely audible. "I know what it's like to lose a parent too soon. My mom passed away as well... She was hit by a car years ago. The jerk who ran her over didn't even stop to help her. And no one witnessed it... or maybe they did, but no one cared enough to get involved. A little while later, on the same road, a famous actor got hit... and guess what? Hundreds of witnesses."

"That's horrible..." Fiamma says, at a loss for words. She knows better than anyone that nothing can really be said in moments like these.

Lorenzo continues, lost in his memories. "The crash was so violent that my mom was thrown a good distance. The headlight shape was stamped into her right leg, almost like a tattoo. I was at school when it happened. I remember the teacher coming over to me, gently patting my head. She looked at me like I was the unluckiest kid on the planet, and then took me to the principal's office. My grandmother was already there, her eyes red and puffy. She kept blowing her nose. My memories after that are foggy, just bits and pieces, like images that barely make sense. But I remember the last time I saw my mom clearly. She was in a light brown coffin. I was wearing a dark suit, something that made me look like an idiot, like I was wearing someone else's clothes. I never asked whose they were. I don't even know why they put me in that suit. All I remember is looking at my mom's body. It seemed so small, lying in that coffin, wrapped in silk. It felt like it lasted only a few minutes, but maybe it was longer, maybe an hour... I have no idea. But I do remember thinking, almost obsessively, That's not my mom. It's hard to explain, but I knew it wasn't her, not in that cold, stiff body that was already starting to change. I didn't know where she was, but I knew she wasn't there."

"I get it," says Fiamma, noticing how Lorenzo's voice is trembling. "I have fuzzy memories too... I remember the good times when he was alive, but the whole time he was sick is a blur. I don't really remember the day he passed either. Just a few scattered images..."

"Maybe it's better to forget some things," Lorenzo says, his voice now steady and almost philosophical. "I read somewhere that the brain has a way of protecting us from particularly traumatic moments. It's like a defense mechanism. It clears out the memories we don't need, so we only remember the things we can handle."

"Maybe that's what happened to me…" Fiamma nods. "But it doesn't always feel right. I mean, it's an important part of my life. Even if it was awful and painful, it's still who I am. It's like there's something missing, and I feel like I need to find it, somewhere deep inside me. Like I need to take back that piece of my life that was taken from me."

"Maybe one day it'll all come back to you. Just like that! Have you thought about it? I do, all the time. But when I do, I also wonder if it's worth it. Remembering, I mean. Who knows? Maybe some things are better left buried, with everything else… maybe the best thing is to just keep moving forward."

Lorenzo pauses, tugs at his sweater cuff, and shrugs before saying, "I've even stopped crying about it. The last time, my tears were so sharp they burned my eyes, like someone squirted lemon juice in them. Even my tears have turned on me. They've gone bad, just like everything else."

The room goes quiet. The only sound is the song *Roads* by Portishead playing softly from two speakers in the living room. Fiamma suddenly realizes it's playing and feels a sharp pang in her chest, but tries to push it aside.

"Your taste in music is a little old-school," she says, trying to lighten the mood. "This was one of my dad's favorite songs. It was pretty famous for a while…"

"Well, I guess your dad and my mom had something in common after all, at least musically. This was one of her favorites. But the CD belongs to Roberto."

"Sorry… I didn't mean to sound like I was criticizing," Fiamma quickly apologizes.

"Don't worry about it," Lorenzo reassures her, though

his expression is hard to read. "But honestly, I think you're luckier than I am. I mean, maybe lucky isn't the right word, but at least you had a chance to say goodbye to your dad and come to terms with losing him. My biggest regret is that I never got to say goodbye to my mom. The fact that she died instantly was a blessing, I guess… because at least she didn't suffer, or at least not for long. For me, though, the trauma was massive. One minute, everything's fine, and the next, she's gone. At least you had time to say goodbye and prepare yourself…"

"What the hell are you talking about?" Fiamma's face turns bright red. "Lucky? Really? You think it was easier for me? Have you ever watched someone die from cancer? Have you seen someone go through all the chemo, the radiation, the endless pills? Have you watched someone you love wither away before your eyes, day after day? I don't think so. So here's what it's like when you watch someone you love die from cancer: You see them lose everything, slowly. You watch them change in horrible ways, and there's nothing you can do about it. In just a few days, I saw my dad go from this vibrant, strong person to someone barely holding on, ready to give up. He was my hero, the one who could conquer the world with a smile. And I saw him turn into a pile of bones, begging to be put to sleep. Do you think it was easy? No. It wasn't."

Fiamma realizes the words have spilled out in a rush, one after the other. She suddenly feels like she can't breathe and takes a deep breath, trying to steady herself. She looks directly at Lorenzo, who is staring down, visibly shaken.

"I'm so sorry…" Lorenzo says after a long pause, his voice barely a whisper, "I didn't mean… I didn't mean to…"

Fiamma knows her reaction was over the top. "No, I'm sorry," she says, softer this time. "I was too harsh… What I wanted you to understand is that there's no Richter scale for pain. You can't compare whose suffering is worse. It doesn't work that way. Do you understand?"

*

"Do you want to talk about your mom?" Fiamma almost whispers the question, as though speaking softly might make it less painful. "I mean… whatever you remember about her, even if it's just a little bit."

"Of course, I'd like that," Lorenzo responds with a gentle smile, understanding her hesitation and offering her reassurance.

"My memories of my mom are kind of… all over the place," he continues, glancing at the light coming through his glass of white wine.

"Take this wine, for example. I can still remember what her favorite wine was. Not that she drank a lot of it… she wasn't really into drinking. She couldn't hold her alcohol at all; just a couple of glasses and she'd be tipsy… and kind of funny, too." Lorenzo smiles, clearly amused by the memory. "When she had a little too much, she'd laugh in this totally ridiculous way. It was contagious, and kind of weird. You would've loved it! It was hilarious to watch. This little woman, and suddenly, for no reason at all, she'd burst into this loud, hearty laugh… If I think about it, I still laugh just remembering it!"

Fiamma can almost feel herself in his memory, seeing Lorenzo and his mother laughing together, her eyes glassy from the wine, her expression slightly vacant, like someone who's had just a little too much. For a moment, she wants to smile at the thought, but a deep sense of sadness fills her instead.

"Refosco dal Peduncolo Rosso," Lorenzo says slowly, rolling the words around in his mouth. "That was her favorite wine. Pretty cool name, right? It's so unique and fun, it'd be impossible to forget it. I'm not even sure if she liked it more for the taste or the name itself. I remember she even made up a little story: The tale of King Refosco, a poor kid with bright red hair like hers, who one day became king, because..." Lorenzo pauses, staring into space, as if trying to hold onto a fading memory. "Wait, let me think... oh yeah, it was because of his little ponytail, like a red stem, hanging at the back of his neck, making him stand out from all the other kids. The king didn't have any heirs, so he chose this odd little boy as his successor, from that strange little town. King Refosco dal Peduncolo Rosso."

"That's a sweet story!" Fiamma exclaims. "I would've loved to meet your mom... she must've been so creative."

"She was... she really was. And she was also incredibly sweet." Lorenzo's eyes darken, and Fiamma feels the sadness returning. She's about to say something, but he beats her to it. "I've forgotten so much about her. That wine story is one of the few things I can still remember clearly. And sometimes I feel so stupid for that. It's like my mind just decided to block out most of her image, maybe to protect me... I don't know. I've forgotten the smell of her skin, for example. And yet, I remember how that scent always stood out when she'd hug me. I've forgotten the exact color of her eyes. I know they were green... but what kind of green? Was it like fresh grass, or green apples, or the sea, or dark bottle green? I can't remember. And none of the photos I have of her help, either. Not one of them is close enough or clear enough to remind me. In most of the pictures, she's looking away or down, probably because she hated having her picture taken."

"I've forgotten how her voice sounded, too. The only thing I remember is that she said the letter 'S' in this special way, like it got stuck for a second between her front teeth, making this soft hissing sound, like she was trying to make sure she was noticed. I don't remember which hand she used to push that strand of hair off her face, though I can still see the movement... the way her red hair, kind of like yours but darker, fell over a bunch of freckles on her face. I remember her hand gently brushing it away, slow and careful, but I can't remember if it was her right hand or her left one. You might think, 'What's the big deal?' but to me, it matters. Every little piece of her that's missing from my memory, it drives me crazy. I keep trying to put the puzzle back together, trying to figure out when I started losing so many memories of her."

"I've got some pretty mixed-up memories of my dad too," Fiamma says, noticing that Lorenzo's eyes are filled with tears and his voice is trembling. She reaches out, trying to comfort him.

"I remember so little about the last days of his illness. Just these hazy, blurry images. I remember his hospital room, that awful smell of disinfectant that sometimes reminded me of the bathrooms at school, or the smell of cat urine. I remember a box of tissues on the tray next to his bed. I remember him sitting there with a bib around his neck, and thinking how funny it looked, because I hadn't worn one of those in years. I remember the look in his eyes when he saw me, this flash of happiness mixed with sadness, maybe even shame. And I remember that my dad would cry every time he saw me. He didn't say a word or shed any tears, but he was crying inside."

Lorenzo seems distant now, his gaze fixed on something far away, unreachable.

"My mom died in the fall, and whenever I think about it, I always see the color orange. I wasn't there when it happened, but I know the paramedics were wearing bright orange uniforms, so loud, like they were screaming at you. I remember this little orange pumpkin spilling out of one of the plastic bags she brought home from the market. And all around, the trees and the ground were covered in orange leaves. Leaves without life, just like her."

Fiamma decides to pull Lorenzo back from his distant thoughts. She reaches for his arm, gently trying to bring him back.

"What about your dad? Was he there for you?"

Lorenzo squints as if he's trying to block out distractions, focusing on a single memory. "I remember when I was with my grandma at the headmaster's office. My dad called me from the hospital… He was cursing and telling me that my mom was gone for good. He said she was an idiot for getting hit by a car, like some dumb cat, and that it was just gonna be me and him from now on. My dad's not exactly a gentleman… I remember his yelling, but I never understood what pissed him off more, the fact that he wouldn't have her to yell at anymore, or that she wouldn't be around to do his laundry."

Fiamma's eyes widen in shock at his words. There's so much resentment in Lorenzo's voice when he talks about his father.

"The first thing I did when I was alone in the house?" Lorenzo continues, nervously twisting his wrist. "I went into the living room... My mom had a set of crystal glasses she never used. She was obsessed with them. She'd always say that crystal is beautiful but delicate, and you had to handle it carefully. She used to wash those glasses all the time, just to keep the dust off and make them shine. She'd fill the sink with warm water, soak them one at a time for five minutes, then wash them gently with soap, inside and out. Afterward, she'd rinse them and leave them upside down on a dish towel to dry."

"She never wanted to use them, though. She said she was saving them for a special occasion, like when I graduated. 'You'll be the first in the family to get a degree,' she'd say. 'Then we'll have something to celebrate!'"

"Well, the day she passed, I took those glasses and dropped them, one by one. The sound they made when they shattered was almost pleasant. Like raindrops on metal. Seriously, it was almost musical. The pieces went everywhere, like they were trying to run away. I didn't cry. I just watched them break, mesmerized. But when the last one hit the floor, I couldn't hold it in anymore. I just broke down."

Fiamma watches Lorenzo shudder as he recalls the moment. She puts a comforting hand on his shoulder, her voice full of concern.

"Are you okay?" she asks softly.

"Yeah… yeah, I'm fine. Sorry, I shouldn't have gone down memory lane like that… Your turn now: what did you do after your dad passed?"

"I… I don't really remember much about what happened after, except for crying. But I do remember how I would try to imagine a different version of things, like if I could change the last chapter of my life. I would picture my dad getting better, the chemo working, and him coming home. I imagined us throwing him a big celebration, with a cake we made ourselves, waiting for him and grandma. It made me feel lighter when I thought that way, but reality hit and the sadness just came back, stronger than before."

Fiamma hesitates, her eyes lowering, feeling vulnerable. She can barely speak the words when Lorenzo's question cuts through her thoughts.

"Have you ever thought back on your father's death and felt such overwhelming grief that you thought you'd die too? Or acted in a way you later regretted?"

She stares at him, her heart racing, unsure how to respond. It feels as though he can see right through her, and she suddenly feels exposed.

"There have been many times," she says slowly, choosing her words carefully, "many times, even now. Practically every day," she adds, her voice dropping to a whisper. She can't bear to meet his eyes now.

"I can't talk about it right now. I'm sorry…"

I should feel uncomfortable in this room. In this house that isn't mine, whose owner I don't even know. This house where I have no right to be, a place that feels less like home than a hotel room. But he's here too. He moves slowly and gently on top of me, almost as if he's gliding over me. Sometimes his trembling hand brushes against me, while the other one caresses my hair. I can't look him in the eyes, but I can hear his heart beating in sync with his quickening breath.

In this room that doesn't belong to us, there are three of us: me, him, and the moonlight that pours through the windows and paints our bodies. We shed our clothes and slipped into an illusion. We hung our thoughts on the bedpost and scattered our fears across the floor, in a tangle of cotton and sweat. I watch his hand on my stomach, the silver tones on his pale skin. I lie on my side, and he's behind me, mirroring my position. Our backs are turned to the door, closing out the rest. The outside world is gone. All the sounds, the noise, the lies, the plans. The emptiness, the stench, the perfumes. Everything we've lived through, everything we've endured before we met. Everything that existed before we found each other. Before us. We're two lost people, trying to lose ourselves in the illusion of finding each other. He moves his hand from my stomach, sliding it upward, tracing an imaginary S on my skin, until it reaches my hair. He caresses each strand slowly, as if we have all the time in the world. My hair feels endless under his touch, slipping through his fingers as he gently twirls it at the tips. It feels beautiful under his silent gaze. For a moment, I feel beautiful too, lying on this bed that seems suspended in mid-air, bathed in moonlight. If it were up to him, we'd stay like this for hours, studying each other like scared animals reunited after a long chase through brambles, drenched in adrenaline, blood, and anger, wary and wounded, exhausted from a pointless fight. But tonight, I don't feel afraid. I have the reckless courage of someone who's already lost so much and has nothing left to lose, nothing to expect. I turn toward him, take his face in my trembling hands, trying to keep them steady. I caress his skin, kissing it more urgently now. I kiss every inch of him, tasting his body, creating tiny, imaginary wounds that only I can heal. I offer him pieces of my world, my lips, my skin, my hands, my pleasure.

When he enters me, I think that it would be amazing to keep him here forever. And for a few endless minutes, it feels like maybe I can forget everything. I feel nothing but this moment.

I don't think about the darkness I've hidden in for so long.

I don't think about the invisible scars I carry inside.

I don't think about the lies that surround me.

I don't think about the wounds I inflict on myself each day.

I think only about this tiny, fleeting moment of happiness, this gift that someone is giving me. That I'm giving myself, for the first time. My first real time.

In this room that doesn't belong to us.

In this room, we are just two. Through the crack in the door, I can hear the notes of Lou Reed's Perfect Day. Outside the window, the moon is shaped like a crescent, scratching at the black sky and sliding across the piano keys and strings. The music glides over the slick surface of this night I wish would never end, scraping away the last fragments of silence that still separate us. In this room that doesn't belong to us, I am alone. The moonlight is chased away by the first rays of dawn, and he has already drifted into sleep. I watch him, and I notice his breathing, it's slow and rhythmic, but sometimes it turns into a sigh, deep and wide. I wonder where he goes then… what he dreams then. For a moment, I think I'd like to latch onto one of those breaths and fall asleep with him. But the silence in this strange room is too precious to waste. I savor every drop, imprinting it on my mind and body. I will become silence too, when I leave, so I don't wake him. Yes, I'll slip away quietly, hand in hand with the dawn that's breaking.

On her way home, Fiamma feels exposed and defenceless. It's not so much because it's dawn, and she's walking alone through the empty streets of Rome, but because for the first time in her life, she's given someone something far more significant and deeper than just her body. Lorenzo has revealed a part of her she'd never shown anyone before, maybe not even herself. He's gone deeper than she ever intended. And he did so without inflicting any physical harm. But the pain Fiamma feels now is one that digs much deeper, spanning years, months, days, and nights, reaching into places she's not sure she wants anyone to access. The pain she feels now has no name, and perhaps no clear explanation. It's a pain that mixes joy, fear, uncertainty, and melancholy. A quiet, reserved pain that hides in a corner of her heart, only raising its head now and then to remind her it's still there, just to make sure she doesn't forget. Fiamma is about to put the key in the lock when she feels her phone vibrating in her pocket. It's a message from Lorenzo, perfectly timed, and it pulls a smile from her, momentarily distracting her from the selfish pain that's afraid of being left behind.

A bed open to the nothingness of a closed door/ the dawn spread across a sky empty of stars/ I, drunken with caresses/ on this empty bed/ like a bottle shattered by your absence.

Still on her doorstep, Fiamma sends a quick, nervous reply to Lorenzo, matching her mood in the moment:

A poem... should I be scared? ;)

His response comes quickly, making her smile again:

I should've been the one scared, when I woke up and you weren't next to me... wasn't the best wake-up, you know? Plus, you didn't even have the excuse of a carriage turning into a pumpkin... and you didn't leave me a single slipper! :)

Fiamma thinks for a moment, trying to come up with a funny, clever reply that might make him laugh too. But all she can think of is a simple, dull, and boring *Sorry*. She feels stupid and immediately regrets it, wishing she hadn't just sent those two words. A few minutes later, her phone vibrates again, and she receives another long message:

Don't apologize... in any case, you're still here. You're still lying on this bed. You're still with me. And our pleasure is still here, woven into the threads of these sheets. My longing for you is in every part of me, between my lashes, like a memory of salt. I wrap myself in it, and I feel it's never enough, as if it's always winter here. As if the cold isn't outside me, but inside. You're still here, in this moment, and forever.

She finishes reading the message for the second time, savoring every word slowly, when the phone vibrates again.

P.S. The poem, no matter how silly and trite, was written with a lot of passion by a certain Lorenzo Ebano. A half-crazy guy who's decided to travel the world on a red motorcycle and who's completely lost his mind over a very special redhead.

Fiamma types her reply while lying on her bed, physically drained but mentally wide awake:

That Lorenzo you're talking about isn't half-crazy... he's completely crazy. Especially since he's fallen for a strange and complicated girl. Come on, *poet*, you should get some rest!

His hands play cracked keys of notes and threads
to dig deep inside me.
They probe, tearing at my soul,
dressing my wounds
with words that unravel and heal.
His fingers move along the edges of scars never fully closed,
peering over chasms of hope,
gazing down without ever falling.
His fingertips tremble
on my skin, with every pulse and wave of pleasure,
brushing against emptiness, painting it with shadows,
clinging to the final ray of light
balanced on the belly of the night.

This is definitely not the reaction Fiamma was expecting.

She's just finished talking to Elife on the phone. She told her about the night she spent with Lorenzo, the magic between them, his tenderness, his dawn messages, how happy she feels, but also how lost and scared she is. She's on top of the world and yet teetering on the edge of a cliff. After a few minutes of non-stop talking, Fiamma starts to sense an unusual silence on the other end, awkward and unsettling.

"Eli, are you there?"

Fiamma pulls the phone away from her ear and looks at it, double-checking to make sure the call's still going. A voice, almost unfamiliar, reassures her that the line is still open. But it doesn't bring her any comfort. "Yeah, I'm here. I'm listening…"

It's Elife's voice, but it sounds distant, almost robotic, and Fiamma can barely recognize it.

"Oh…okay. I thought maybe you passed out or fell asleep or something," she says, trying to keep things light. She furrows her brow. "Is everything okay?"

"Yeah, it's fine." The same distant, mechanical tone.

"Okay… but… I mean… don't you have anything to say? No reaction, no advice, nothing? I feel a little ridiculous, like I've been talking to myself for the last five minutes!"

"Well, you're right about that," Elife replies, her voice flat and lifeless. "I'd say you've been delivering a monologue. *Monologue*, from the Greek word *monólogos* (mónos, 'alone,' and lógos, 'speech'), is a speech delivered by one person…”

“Eli, stop.” Fiamma snaps, her patience running out. “I couldn't care less about the etymology of ‘monologue,’ and I don't care if you agree with me about the word I used! What the hell, El? I'm just asking you to actually *engage* for once! And what's with that robotic tone? It's like I'm talking to a machine!”

Fiamma feels a rush of emotion. She's like a dam breaking, there's no stopping her now. “Are you even my best friend? I don't know if your dictionary or that crazy computer in your head has space for what friendship means, but it's about sharing. Sharing joy, sharing pain, every moment. Right now, I'm trying to share with you, my *best* friend, the joy of finally meeting someone who makes me feel good. And in return, I expect a reaction. A *human* reaction. I'm not asking you to jump up and down, do a happy dance, or anything crazy, but at least show me you're happy for me. That's all. I don't think it's too much to ask.”

“You're right, Fiamma…”

That voice again. Familiar, but still cold, distant, mechanical. It fills Fiamma with a mix of fear and sadness. “In fact, the reaction you expect from a best friend is exactly what you described…” Elife continues. “But, unfortunately, at this moment, I can't give that to you. I'm really sorry. I wish I could, but I just can't.” Silence falls, heavy and awkward.

“I'm sorry I can't fulfill that need right now, and that I can't make you happy in the way Lorenzo does. I just can't. But I do hope you'll be happy. I really hope your happiness grows, every single day. I truly mean it. I wish you all the happiness in the world.”

Girls my age usually cover their walls with posters of their favorite singers, bands, or actors. A few might have a giant picture of that super talented, incredibly good-looking dancer. The younger ones typically go for images of famous cartoon characters. As for me, I only have one poster in the tiny apartment I live in: a reproduction of Nighthawks, probably Edward Hopper's most famous painting.

Nighthawks shows a scene inside a diner: a couple sitting at the counter, a bartender, and another customer sitting off to the side with his back to us. When Hopper talked about this piece, he said that, unconsciously, he was trying to capture the loneliness of a big city at night, with its empty streets and a silence so deep it feels almost metaphysical. Personally, I think he nailed it, the poem of silence and the loneliness that's present in every big city.

A lot of people find this painting endlessly sad, but for me, it fills my nights. Sometimes, just looking at it or even thinking about it hanging there on my wall when everything else is dark, makes me feel less alone.

Eli gave me that poster last Christmas, and now that it's been two days since we last spoke, since we haven't exchanged even a text message, that little piece of paper has taken on even more meaning. Sometimes I look at it and wish I could step right into the scene, order a dark beer from the bartender, and strike up a conversation with the only other people there. I'd ask them what went wrong, if they could help me patch things up with my best friend.

Then I remember: we didn't really have a fight. We just stopped talking out of nowhere, for no clear reason. She let me down, and I... I hurt her (I could tell from her voice that she was hurting), but I don't even know how. The other day, in a fit of anger, I told her off, thinking we'd sort it out face-to-face later. But when I went to school, she wasn't there *before or after class. She wasn't waiting for me like she usually does. Now, for two days, she's been avoiding my calls, and won't respond to my texts. I don't know what to do, or what to think anymore. All I know is I miss her more than anything, and I feel completely lost without her. The happiness I've been feeling with Lorenzo just feels shallow now, it's like it's missing something, clipped at the wings. How can I be fully happy without my best friend by my side to share it with?*

"Hey, do you wanna come with me to a steampunk party? It's organized by some people I met on a website for genre enthusiasts. It should turn out to be fun! Of course, you'll have to make the effort to dress appropriately for the event!"

Lorenzo feels a bit guilty dampening Fiamma's excitement with a response that's more confused than enthusiastic. "Oh, uh... I don't really know much about steampunk, honestly..."

"Neither did I know much about sushi! But I came to your dinner, and I had a great time. Anyway, there's really nothing hard about it; you just have to learn to see the world around you with different eyes. For the clothes, you can even use a lot of recycled stuff. You don't have to spend money, quite the opposite! People recycle all sorts of things: broom handles, pipes, springs, even gears from old clocks."

"Okay... so if I get stuck, maybe I'll take a trip to the recycling center!" jokes Lorenzo.

"Exactly! That's the spirit! Though I seriously doubt you'll need to go to the recycling center... Anyway, you have plenty of time to get ready; the party's next week. Oh, by the way, I'll give you a super useful tip I read online: to 'age' accessories and make them more authentic, you can use liquid bitumen. I think you can find it at art stores. You just use a dry brush on metal, leather, glass, etc., to give the object a worn look. Cool, huh?"

"Yeah, sure... super cool!" Lorenzo raises his eyebrows and grimaces in an ironic way. "But most importantly...

this is definitely going to be a breeze to prepare for!"

*

The song *Steampunk Revolution* by Abney Park blares at full volume as they enter. The old warehouse, abandoned for who knows how many years, seems to come back to life. The event organizers have cleaned it up, set up the audio system, the lights, a small bar with the basics, and even a projector showing the music video. The end result is perfectly in line with the steampunk philosophy. It feels like they're in a place suspended in time, surrounded by details that recall the past mixed with technological elements that are decidedly more modern. Lorenzo looks around, fascinated and amazed. He's done his best to not stick out among the flood of top hats, welding goggles, baroque shirts, tiered skirts, bow ties, and tailcoats. With limited funds, he asked Roberto for help with the clothes. Thanks to him, he managed to get a white lace-trimmed shirt discarded from a fashion show in Tuscany, a black leather waistcoat, and a colonial helmet, on which he added a pair of welding goggles. He even managed to craft a kind of manometer using an old tuna can, a small tube, and a piece of clear plastic from a bottle. Fiamma watches his look out of the corner of her eye, it's a mix of a mad scientist, a dandy, and an explorer, and she fights back a smile. Lorenzo also glances sideways at Fiamma: she's more beautiful than ever tonight. For the occasion, she's wearing her favorite jacket, a red Victorian-style one with black lace details. It's an asymmetrical design, longer in the back, embellished with ruffles and a bow, with long, wide sleeves and black rose-shaped buttons. Lorenzo can't help but think they're simply stunning, both she and the jacket.

135

"Shall we go grab a drink?" he suggests after a brief hesitation.

"We're here to get totally wasted, so, yeah, let's start drinking!" Fiamma replies enthusiastically, yelling to be heard over the loud Abney Park music and other background noises.

"I thought we were here to have fun… Anyway, okay…"

Lorenzo's voice gets drowned out by the surrounding noises and by Fiamma's firm grip as she drags him toward the already crowded bar. About thirty minutes later, Lorenzo realizes that Fiamma wasn't joking: her main goal at this party seems to be getting drunk. In just a few minutes, she's already downed several vodka Red Bulls, at a speed and with an eagerness that's decidedly out of the ordinary. She hasn't even noticed, or maybe she's pretending not to notice, the stunned look on Lorenzo's face every time she orders a new drink.

"Man, you drink more than a sailor!" Lorenzo jokes, trying to hide his embarrassment and amazement at seeing her down another glass. Fiamma finishes drinking and then fixes him with two red, glassy eyes. She tries to stay as steady as possible on her feet, but ends up swaying noticeably, alternating weight between her right and left foot.

"I've had bulimia since I was fourteen…" she suddenly says, after a long silence, her voice thick from alcohol. She says these nine words out of nowhere, as casually as if she were talking about the weather or commenting on something random. This completely shocks Lorenzo, who remains frozen with his plastic cup half full of light beer, as if something has paralyzed him. He has no words to respond, only staring at Fiamma with wide, blank eyes.

"I don't just overdo it with alcohol… I overdo everything I can swallow. I remember my first time. The first time I made myself throw up, I mean. I also remember my first time, let's say, as a woman. Though back then I wasn't much of a woman, since I was still a kid. He… my mom's partner… Giorgio… came into my room and did whatever he wanted. Just like that. While my mom was sleeping. At that time, mom was taking sleeping pills and would fall into a deep sleep, like a rock. As for me, I've always had very light sleep, I wake up at the slightest noise. Thinking about it now, I really hope my mom never noticed anything. I want to believe that's why she never intervened or ended that nightmare."

Lorenzo can't bring himself to say anything or move a muscle. For a moment, it feels like he's stopped breathing entirely.

"It went on for years, that nightmare, you know? It went on in silence. The silence he imposed on me, the silence of the night, the silence of a house that was too big and my room was too far from the rest. That silence continued until I found the strength to end it. One night, like any other, I simply found the courage to scream all my hatred at that bastard. I screamed it softly, so I wouldn't completely break the silence surrounding us. So I wouldn't wake up my mom. But I screamed it, in my way, with clenched teeth, and with my eyes. I spat all the contempt I had for him over those years of abuse. I threatened him with a strength I didn't know I had."

Fiamma stares into Lorenzo's eyes, her gaze watery. She's not drunk enough to miss the fact that he's completely shaken, unable to speak a single word. That new revelation has drained him of any ability to react, freezing his movements and leaving his face in a stunned expression, making him look like a mannequin in a horror movie.

"Since that night, he never came back to bother me, but after a while, another nightmare started for me. A different one, but no less terrible, bulimia. I've been fighting it for five years. Honestly, I'm not sure 'fighting' is the right word. I haven't done anything to fight it, really. I know it's a serious disorder, and I know I'm different from a lot of girls my age who don't have it, but I've never done anything to get rid of it. I've never told anyone. You're the first person I've ever told. My best friend Eli doesn't even know. I don't think I could handle one of her usual know-it-all reactions, full of facts, statistics, and scientific study results. And anyway… I'm not even sure we're still friends, you know? We haven't talked in days. I don't know what's going on with her. Maybe I've lost her forever. Who knows! After all, I'm destined to lose the people I love… Maybe something's wrong with me…"

"Why did you choose me?" Lorenzo suddenly shakes off his temporary stupor and looks at her with a questioning gaze. "Why did you decide to tell me this secret, right now?"

"Why I chose you… Good question. Too bad I don't have an answer. Maybe it's simply because I'm drunk enough to open up to someone. Or maybe it's because I feel even lonelier than usual. And I'm really scared of dying. I've been bulimic for five years, you get it? Five long years. I'm basically a time bomb, ready to explode any second. I already have stomach problems and suffer from heart arrhythmias; if I keep going like this, I might develop dangerous kidney, endocrine, and lung issues. Not to mention a possible esophageal rupture. And an even more extreme consequence, which you can imagine."

"So, you've told me because you're asking for help, right? You want me to help you in some way…"

Lorenzo's question is met with a long silence as Fiamma desperately tries to avoid his gaze. Her eyes dart back and forth, as if searching for something to hold on to. Or a way out.

"I don't even know, honestly. It's hard to explain, but even though I'm fully aware of the risks, the idea of getting rid of bulimia scares me."

"It scares you?! Wait… Sorry, maybe I didn't hear that right… You're scared of fixing this problem?"

"Yeah. Like I said, it's hard to explain, especially to someone who's never dealt with bulimia nervosa. Or with anything remotely like it, really. It's like… if I got better, I'd lose something. I wouldn't have that outlet anymore. It's been part of my life for so long that the idea of a 'normal' life without it feels… unbearable."

"That doesn't make any sense…"

"Maybe not to you! Because you have no idea what I'm talking about."

Fiamma only realizes she's yelling when people nearby start turning to look. She doesn't care, but lowers her voice anyway, still speaking with the same bitter edge. "What do you know about what makes sense or not? Just standing there like a statue, telling me I'm not making sense. Who the hell do you think you are? If I hadn't opened up to you the way I did, maybe I'd get it, but saying it doesn't make sense? That's awful. Even worse than Eli. You think you know everything. You don't know shit about what I've been through. Yeah, you lost your mom, fine. She got hit by a car. It's tragic, but it happens. A lot of people lose a parent. I did too."

Her last words come out as a whisper. They lose strength the second they leave her lips, dripping with bitterness, self-disgust. She wishes she could erase them, like chalk off a blackboard. But it's too late.

The hurt and disbelief on Lorenzo's face say it all.

"God, I hope it's the alcohol talking… Because if it's not, then you're just being cruel. And you have the nerve to lecture me about being sensitive? What is this… some kind of trauma competition? You want to compare pain? See who had the shittier life? Great. Be ready to lose."

Fiamma's silence, and the guilt written all over her, only push Lorenzo to keep going. His voice is steadier now, more cutting.

"Fine. You want to know my story? Let's do this. Let's make tonight the night for ugly truths. I'll tell you a love story, my parents' love story. They got married young, broke as hell. But it didn't matter to them. They would've lived on the street as long as they could be together. Hand in hand. Always. Sharing everything, body, soul, blood. My mom met my dad when she was your age. She got pregnant, had to walk down the aisle, and hear my maternal grandparents say, 'Take responsibility now, whore.'

"I am 'lucky' enough not to remember my grandparents… they both died when I was still a toddler. But from what my mom and aunt told me, I know enough. Truth is, I think my mom just jumped into my dad's arms to escape a shitty home. Too bad she went from bad to worse. Once they got married, the fairytale ended. Prince Charming turned into a monster. My dad was a violent drunk, possessive as hell. So they lived 'unhappily ever after,' like some kind of backward fairy tale. Tragic. Absurd."

Fiamma senses what's coming. She looks horrified. "I'm so sorry, Lorenzo, I…"

But Lorenzo either doesn't hear her or pretends not to. He's somewhere else now, trapped in his memories.

"You talk about silence, how Giorgio hurt you in the quiet of that huge house at night, your bedroom too far from your mom's. My past was the opposite. It was loud. Full of my dad's drunken rages. My mom's screams. Her begging him to stop. I remember the sound of furniture crashing, chairs slamming into walls, plates smashing on the floor. Bottles flung like javelins, hitting anything, or anyone, in their path. Usually my mother.

I'd find her curled up, trying to shield herself."

He pauses for breath. His eyes lock with Fiamma's. She's almost pleading now. Nearly in tears.

"Do you know what a beating sounds like? Whether it's you being hit, or the person you love most in the world? Let me tell you. It's deafening. It's unbearable. A beating sounds like the bruises you'll do anything to hide: layers of clothes, even in the heat of summer. It sounds like lies and fake smiles, saying 'I'm fine' when deep down, they're screaming 'Please help me, before it's too late.' Noise ruled my life. Not silence. When my dad wasn't home and things were calm, my mom would sing. She was Spanish, lively, fun. She didn't care if she was out of tune or forgot the lyrics. She was goofy and beautiful all at once. Every time I hear *Hoy* by Gloria Estefan, her favorite, I see her again. Singing into a broom like it's a microphone. That song hits me with a storm of feelings, sadness, joy, anger. My mom could fill any room with life, with her voice, with her energy, despite everything else. No, my life wasn't quiet. The only silence I remember, and hated, was the silence from the neighbors. Not once, in all those years, did they speak up. Not a word. Not even an anonymous call to the cops. Nothing. Maybe they were scared. Or maybe they just didn't care. And when my mom died, then they came around. Hugging me. Saying they were sorry. Hypocrites. I remember this one neighbor, this nosy woman who knew everyone's business, and I shouted in her face: 'She's finally not suffering anymore. Now go find someone else to gossip about.' God, it felt good to say that. Maybe it was mean. But I don't care."

"It wasn't mean," Fiamma says quietly, finally finding her voice. "It was honest. You found a way to let it out."

"You think so?" Lorenzo raises an eyebrow, still a little wary, but then he cracks a smile. "Let's see… You don't have a dad. I don't have a mom. You had a checked-out mother. I had an abusive father. I'd say we make a pretty solid team, don't you think?"

"Yeah. A pretty solid team of losers…" Fiamma teases.

Lorenzo lifts his finger to her lips to hush her. She looks heartbreakingly beautiful. Just as she's about to say something else, he gently presses his finger there, as if shielding her. Shielding her from her own words. Like shielding your eyes from the sun. Fiamma glows with light, radiant in a way that almost hurts to look at.

With his other hand, Lorenzo pulls her close. They sway together to the haunting melody of *New Albion I* by Paul Shapera.

HEAT

I haven't checked in for a few days, Dad. And I have no excuses. Unless happiness counts as a valid one.

The truth is, things have been going better than usual lately. Actually, I'd say they've been amazing, for the first time in what feels like forever. I finally made peace with Eli, school hasn't been as awful as it usually is, and things with Lorenzo are going great. Opening up to each other at the steampunk party only brought us closer.

In short, I haven't had as many reasons to shut myself away in a room and spill my thoughts onto these pages, the ones I write for you. If you were here, you'd probably arch an eyebrow like you used to when we played, pretending to be mad at me, and with that teasing smirk, you'd say something like, "Oh, I see how it is! You only come to me when you need something… I'm just the guy you turn to when things go wrong, huh?"

Don't take it the wrong way, Dad. And don't think for a second that I don't need you anymore. I still haven't found anyone who could ever take your place, and I doubt I ever will. So please, always be there… and make sure you're right around the corner whenever I need you.

Fiamma's mind is elsewhere. Somewhere far from the books spread out in front of her, miles away from the room where she's supposed to be studying with Elife. It doesn't take long for Eli to notice, her friend's eyes are unfocused, lost in thought.

"Hey! Are you even listening to me?" she finally snaps, slamming her math book onto the desk.

"Yeah, yeah, of course I am…" Fiamma lies, jolting upright.

"Oh, sure. Like hell you are! You really think you can fool me?" Eli isn't in the mood to be messed with. "Listen… I can tell your head's somewhere else, but do you realize that in less than two months, we have finals? You know there's a good chance you won't even hit a passing grade, right? And that's not exactly going to look great. I mean, if you're okay with just scraping by, fine. But I'm telling you, a low score on your diploma could really mess with your future. Unless, of course, you happen to have some especially generous teachers on your side…"

"Oh, no chance. I definitely don't have any generous teachers in my corner," Fiamma cuts in, shaking her head. "In fact, I still have an oral exam left with the philosophy teacher. And she'll shut you down the second you get two answers wrong. My average is only going to tank from here."

"Damn… So you don't even get two chances with her? That's worse than baseball, at least there, you get three strikes before you're out. You're really screwed. So, what are you waiting for? You should be busting your ass studying! I can help you with science and math, since, if I remember right, you absolutely suck at both. But if you don't focus, there's only so much I can do!"

"You're right, Eli… It's just that my mind's somewhere else. Can we take a break?"

"*Another* break? We've been here for two hours and already taken three! At this rate, we'll still be working on this the day after tomorrow."

"I just can't focus right now, Eli…"

Fiamma's pleading expression is enough to make Elife give in.

"Okay… okay, fine. Let's see. First break, we got some air on the balcony while drinking lemonade. Second break, we ate an apple… very, *very* slowly, in tiny slices. Third break, we downed two cups of tea and a whole box of cookies. Hmm, what now? I could entertain you with some random story… Oh! Did I ever tell you how dumb my brother's girlfriend's little brother is? Must be a family trait, since his sister isn't exactly the brightest either. Which is probably why she ended up with my brother… Anyway, the other day, the kid asked me, his exact words, 'If a woman has a tattoo on her stomach and gets pregnant… does the baby come out with colors?' I swear, I had no idea whether to laugh or cry."

"Oh, I would've laughed for sure!" Fiamma snickers. "Then I would've told him yes, the baby is born with a little color exactly where it touched the mother's tattoo. And I'd have added that's how birthmarks happen."

"Well, you're creative. I'm too analytical for that. I just gave him a scientific explanation about why that could never happen. But honestly? I don't think he understood a word I said."

Fiamma is about to reply when her phone buzzes. She

smiles softly at the name on the screen: Lorenzo. But the moment she reads the message, the smile fades. An uneasy feeling creeps in, one she can't quite place.

I need to talk to you. It's about us… Meet me in an hour by the statue in Piazza Pasquino.

Elife barely has time to notice the shift in Fiamma's expression, from happy to unsettled. She doesn't even get the chance to ask what's wrong before her friend starts grabbing her books and backpack, mumbling another rushed, "Sorry, Eli, I have to go," before disappearing out the door.

*

At first, he just stares at her in silence. Then, all at once, he blurts it out: "I'm leaving in a week."

For a second, Fiamma feels like her heart has stopped. In reality, it's only skipped a beat, before racing even faster than before. Much faster.

"What?"

The word barely escapes her lips, caught between uneven breaths.

"I… I don't understand…"

A sigh. Lorenzo looks away, like he's searching for better words, softer words, ones that won't hit quite so hard. He takes a deep breath, but when he exhales, it's just another blast of words.

"Fiamma, what we have is amazing. I've never felt anything like this before." Another sigh, a small break, before Lorenzo goes on.

146

"And I've never opened up to anyone the way I have with you. But I can't just stay in one place. I just can't. I told you that when we met, remember? I was upfront about it from the start... I was fair."

A pause. A heavy, loaded silence, in which Fiamma finds herself latching onto that one word.

Fair.

He was fair. Fair, like playing by the rules, like telling the truth. Fair, because, technically, he warned her. He put it all on the table from day one. And the stupid one, the one who got it wrong, was her.

"I just can't, Fiamma... try to understand."

Lorenzo still won't look at her. His gaze jumps from the marble statue a few feet away to the cobbled street, speckled with spit, broken glass, and gum flattened into the cracks.

He only finds the nerve to meet her eyes when the silence stretches too long, pressing in around them, when she doesn't say a word.

"Fiamma?"

She's been staring at him the whole time, but she hasn't really been seeing him. Instead, she's been watching another version of herself, somewhere, in some other reality, eyes wide in shock, grabbing Lorenzo by the shoulders, shaking him, begging him not to leave her. Some other Fiamma, in some unknown dimension, who actually has the courage to fight back.

"Well? Aren't you gonna say anything?"

Lorenzo's voice reaches her from far away, like through water, but it's enough to pull her out of it.

"Yes..." she whispers, this time looking straight at him.

"Yes, what?" he presses, frowning, his voice edged with frustration and expectation.

"Yes, you're right. You told me the first time we met. You said you never stay in one place too long… You were upfront about it from the start. Or, as you put it, fair."

"And? I mean… don't you have anything else to say? Fiamma… I don't wanna lose you. You have no idea how messed up this is in my head right now! Leaving isn't easy for me, I swear. But I have to. I don't know how we're supposed to make this work with the distance, I have no clue. But I do know I won't forget you. And you? Well? Do you have anything to say?"

There's the slightest tremor in his voice. It's barely there, but Fiamma catches it. And for just a second, a chill runs through her too. Maybe it's the cold. The temperature has dropped out of nowhere in the past few hours, it doesn't feel like late spring anymore. It feels like fall, tipping into winter. The perfect weather for goodbyes.

Fiamma has plenty to say, really. Plenty of arguments to throw at him. But they're buried deep in some corner of that parallel universe, far out of reach.

Here, in this reality, right here, right now, she doesn't have it in her to fight.

She pulls her jacket tighter, turns away, and walks off, leaving Lorenzo standing there, stunned.

Two words.

"Take care."

*

For Fiamma, filling the glass to the brim is the easiest thing in the world. She watches the slow, steady pour, the deep red liquid cascading into the glass. It looks like blood, so much like blood, and it reminds her of that organ, the one that beats inside her chest, small and strong, shaped like a closed fist.

Hurting herself is easy. Fiamma is a pro at it.

The alcohol burns as it slides down her throat, a fiery tongue licking its way to her stomach. It washes everything away, all the dirt, all the excess, until there's nothing left but emptiness. And emptiness is good. Emptiness holds no memories. It erases emotions, dulling them into a single, colorless non-color, one without edges or shades. No gradients of black or white. No flickers of a rainbow.

Emptiness is nothing. And nothingness has no name.

It's a blank sheet of paper, one that can be filled, ripped apart, crumpled, or torn to shreds. A sheet with no expectations. And the best part? Emptiness is easy to fill. All it takes is an endless supply of food.

Fiamma has plenty. There's food everywhere, on the table, near the almost-empty wine bottle, on the sofa bed, on the chair usually buried under dirty clothes. Bags of chips, chocolate bars, snack cakes, candy, cookies, peanuts, pretzels. Enough for a party.

Too bad there is no party. No guests. No reason to celebrate.

Fiamma isn't waiting for anyone. Truth is, she hasn't waited for anything, or anyone, in years. She wouldn't even know how to anymore. And she definitely isn't expecting anything different from a night like this.

As she pours another glass of wine, she thinks about life. About how strange it is, at least, hers. It takes more than it gives. It lets you brush against happiness, just for a second, just long enough to feel it, and then, just like that, it snatches it away, dragging you down, down, down.

And that's exactly what she wants right now.

To sink.

To let go, to keep falling, to slip further and further away from it all.

And as she does, the pain dulls, the pain of the past, the disappointment of the present, the fear of the future.

Everything fades.

Everything drifts away.

And then, after a while, she sees it. Floating in the toilet, next to her body. Like a tiny, broken twig, bobbing in silence.

*

She has no idea what time it is when she picks up her phone and searches for Lorenzo's name. She deliberately ignores the numbers on the screen. If she looked at them, or even glanced out the window, she'd know it's either too late or too early to be calling anyone.

The sky is an undefined color, a mix of white and gray from the fading moon, blended with streaks of yellow and red from the rising sun. But Fiamma doesn't care about the sky or the time. All that matters is that Lorenzo's phone is ringing.

She counts six rings before she hears his groggy voice say her name, his words clinging to a massive question mark.

"Fiamma?"

A rhetorical question that doesn't expect an answer, or maybe one that expects a thousand. What follows is an avalanche of words, hurled at him like shards of glass, ready to slash through anything in their path.

"You're running away, Lorenzo! That's all you do, run. From everything, from everyone. But most of all, from yourself. And you know what? You can't! You can't outrun yourself, do you hear me? Do you? If you don't know that by now, then let me spell it out for you! You can move houses, change cities, change countries, but the shit inside you doesn't just disappear. It sticks to you. It never lets go! And here's something else: You can't run without leaving something behind, without dropping pieces of yourself along the way. Every time you leave a place, you leave a reason to come back. Every time you walk away from someone, part of their soul clings to you, and part of you sticks to them. Forever. Yes, forever. Forever forever forever forever forever! That word terrifies you, doesn't it? It makes you sick. You hate it with everything you've got. It scares you so much you keep moving, thinking that new places, new people, new surroundings will keep you safe from that one damned adverb!"

"You're delirious, Fiamma… Stop it. Just calm down, please." Lorenzo's voice wavers.

"Oh, of course! I'm the crazy one. I'm the one who needs to calm down. Right. I'm just a stupid, bulimic mess who got raped by her stepfather, who has a ghost for a mother and a father who died of cancer. Just some pathetic idiot who drowns herself in booze and food and knows nothing about the world. But you? Oh, you've traveled, haven't you? You know everything, don't you?"

"Please… just stop. Stop…"

If Fiamma could see him, she'd know he looks exactly like his voice sounds, shaking from head to toe, consumed by an uncontrollable tremor.

"Nooo, you stop! You! Do you think you're better than me? Better than everyone else? What are you waiting for? Just go! Run! Get out of here! You sit there, talking to me with that trembling little lamb's voice, and yet I'm the one who's out of her mind? Go on! Leave! Vanish! Disappear! And do me a favor, don't come back. Not ever. Have a nice life!"

The silence that follows is ice cold. Lorenzo feels it, the distance, the sheer emptiness of it. For a moment, he wants to run to her, to hold her, to grip her arms and look into her eyes. He wants to beg her to stop, to stop hurting him, to stop hurting herself. For a moment, he even thinks that maybe he should stay, that maybe, together, they could try to be happy. He wants to tell her she's right. Because for months now, he's been running. From everything, from everyone. With no direction. With no success. With no hope. For years, since his mother died, he's been running from peace itself.

He wants to tell her that a part of him, a huge, overwhelming part of him, wants to stay. To stay and finally make peace with himself.

But the sound of her voice on the phone, distorted by rage, reminds him too much of his father. He remembers that mask of pain and anger. That impenetrable wall of disappointment.

And in that exact moment, Lorenzo makes his decision.

He obeys her.

He turns away, mentally. Slips his phone into his pocket. Walks away, emotionally and in silence, long before he ever packs his bags. Once again, he is running. Running from everything. From everyone.

And most of all, from Fiamma.

And the love he feels for her.

*

Fiamma does what anyone would when they are feeling down: she calls her best friend. She calls Elife and says simply, "I feel horrible. I need to see you."

She hasn't even finished her sentence when she hears Eli reply, "I'll be there in thirty minutes."

Less than twenty-five minutes later, the doorbell rings. One long chime and two short ones, just like always. Their own little Morse code, a silent password they never had to agree on.

Fiamma smiles, because once again, Eli has proven she can always count on her.

As soon as she steps inside, Fiamma wraps her in a tight hug, holding onto her without a word. Eli hugs her back just as fiercely, as if she wants to make them one and the same. The warmth of her embrace is like a breath of fresh air for Fiamma's aching soul, and despite the storm raging inside her, she manages a small smile.

"What happened? What's wrong?" Eli asks after a beat of silence. There's something strange in her expression, something heavy, almost heavier than the sadness pressing down on Fiamma's own heart. For a moment, an overwhelming sorrow washes over her, so intense she feels the urge to break down in tears. She barely manages to hold them back, choosing instead to drown them in a flood of words, pouring out as fast as she can.

"Lorenzo's leaving. I think he's going to Barcelona, where he already has another friend, or whatever, waiting to put him up. Another place to cook, another square to play his stupid bottles. He said what we have, or had, was beautiful, but that he's just not the kind of person who can stay in one place for too long, that he has this thing inside him that keeps pushing him to move on, to always be looking ahead, somewhere else. He told me he'll never forget me, that we should stay in touch, that he doesn't want to lose me completely... and a whole lot of other bullshit. Because, honestly, Eli, who does he think he's fooling? I feel like a complete idiot. How could I have fallen for a guy like that? How could I have thought we had something special when, in the end, I don't even really know him? Now I see it was just me, I was the only one in love, the only one who actually cared. Everyone I love either leaves me, like my dad did, or makes a fool of me, like my mom still does. God, I feel so stupid right now... I'm just rambling... That was such a ridiculous thing to say. But my head is spinning, and my heart feels like it's been put through a shredder, and I just feel so awful, and, "

"Stop."

Elife cuts her off with a single word, sharp as ice. It hits Fiamma like a slap. She still has that strange expression, that veil of sadness covering her eyes, but there's something else too, something almost resentful. She looks at her, but it's as if she doesn't see her. Or doesn't want to.

"W-what?"

"I said stop. That's it. I don't want to hear this."

"Eli, what are you talking about? I just told you I feel like crap, that I need you, and you rushed over here to comfort me, so why are you acting like this? What's going on? And what's with that look? It's like you're mad at me!"

"I'm not mad at you."

Eli's tone, her entire demeanor, sends a surge of anger through Fiamma. She just poured her heart out, told her how much pain she's in, and this is how Eli responds? With that sad, almost bitter look and clipped, cryptic answers? For a fleeting second, Fiamma has the urge to punch her, just to see a different expression cross her face. Something real. Something she can understand.

"I'm not mad at you," Eli repeats. "And I'm sorry you're hurting, but if you're looking for comfort over Lorenzo, I'm the last person you should come to."

Now there are two question marks hanging in the air, one of them plastered right across Fiamma's face. She frowns in total confusion.

"And who else am I supposed to go to? You're my best friend! Who else am I supposed to turn to?"

In the span of minutes, her emotions have ricocheted from sorrow to shock to outright fury. No, this isn't just anger. She's livid. And at this point, she wants to do more than punch Eli. She wants to kick her. Hard. How could she? How could she shut her out like this when she needs her the most? But more than anything, what frustrates her is that she doesn't understand why.

Eli is silent now. No more cryptic words, no more clipped phrases. She won't even look her in the eye anymore, her gaze locked on some random spot on the floor. Fiamma has never seen her like this, and it's throwing her completely off balance. For the first time, Eli feels like a stranger, and the thought makes her stomach churn. It's the kind of awkward discomfort you feel when you're stuck in an elevator with someone you don't know. They're standing so close she can still smell her fruity perfume, just like when they hugged a moment ago. But now, instead of comfort, all she feels is unease. For a second, she almost wants to tell her to leave. To get out. To close the door on the stranger standing in front of her. But then a thought creeps in, maybe she's been neglecting Eli since she got involved with Lorenzo. Maybe Eli feels hurt, left out, and that's why she's acting this way.

Yeah. Maybe it's as simple as that.

But if she's really her best friend, shouldn't she understand? Shouldn't she just let it go?

"When I think about losing you, it feels like the ground is caving in beneath my feet."

Eli's voice cuts through Fiamma's thoughts. But she's still staring at the floor.

"I feel this sudden emptiness in my chest, this

deafening noise in my head, like I'm losing my mind."

"Eli, what are you talking about? Why would you lose me?"

Fiamma steps closer, gently grabs her arm, hoping to break her trance and pull her out of whatever she's seeing on the floor. It works. Elife looks up. Her eyes lock onto Fiamma's. For a moment, they're cold, glassy, like ice. Then the ice gives way to sadness, warmth, and finally a rush of words: "I'm scared I'm going to lose you because what I feel for you isn't the same as what you feel for me. Maybe it never was. And the truth is... I haven't been honest. I haven't been real with you. I can't keep pretending...not to you, and not to myself. I don't think we can stay friends. I don't think it's fair."

"Eli...?"

Three letters hanging in the air after a long, aching pause. A name, a question, a plea.

Now it's Fiamma who feels afraid. A chill runs through her, and she lets go of Elife's arm.

"Do you remember when we talked about our dads' funerals?"

Elife's voice is distant, like a bell caught between chimes.

"You told me what you hated most was how everyone wanted to hug you. How strangers kept giving you comfort you didn't ask for, whispering 'poor sweet girl, my condolences' every time they held you. You said you didn't know what felt worse: hearing a word you didn't even understand back then, or the hugs that felt even colder than the words."

"I remember saying it was the same for me. Too many people. Too much noise. Everyone saying that same empty word, like it was a secret password that unlocked some door to a place I didn't want to go. Some kind of magic spell. And once they said it, they'd hug you. And you couldn't escape. I'm sure I've told you more than once, I hate being touched. Especially after my dad died. Ever since that day, I can't stand it. I just can't."

She pauses, takes a breath, and continues.

"But with you... if you were to hug me now, or tomorrow, or whenever... I'd never feel that way. I'd never want to pull away. I'd never want to run. When you're close, when I feel your warmth beside me, for a little while, I feel completely happy. Totally, absolutely happy."

She falls quiet again. A longer pause this time. Silence hovering in the space between them.

Elife is watching her, eyes searching Fiamma's. There's still a flicker of fear there. One mouth is soft and still, the other opens into a breath, a whisper. And then they touch, just barely, a kiss suspended in time. A kiss like a moment floating between a question and an answer.

"I'm here now..." Elife murmurs, just as their lips part. "I've always been here. And I always will be. But he's gone. He left you."

Her voice sounds far away, like it traveled light years to reach Fiamma, though she's standing right there.

Another pause. Another silence hanging in the air like something sacred. Fiamma's eyes fill with something wordless: tenderness, grief, longing, maybe even love.

"I'm in love with you, Fiamma. I'm saying it, just in case it wasn't clear."

Her words drift like soap bubbles, delicate, weightless, ready to pop.

The ice Fiamma had seen in Elife's eyes a moment ago has melted into water, laced with salt, clinging to the edges of her lashes.

"Eli..."

That name again, barely a whisper. Fiamma's voice trembles. She's no longer afraid, but it feels like a massive weight has dropped onto her shoulders.

"Eli..."

She says it again, softly, stunned, as Elife turns away without a word.

"Eli!"

One last time. A cry, a prayer, a final plea. Her name, stretched into an exclamation that's full of wonder but drained of strength.

And just like that, Fiamma watches her best friend walk away. Silent. Past the heavy door. Away from her trembling lips and into the stillness beyond.

Elife's confession hit me like a ton of bricks, Dad. I felt so stupid. Stupid and mean. Because in all this time, I hadn't known a thing about her. Because I was totally blind, only concerned about myself. Because I never asked her how she was really feeling. Because I ignored her while I was with Lorenzo. And because I realized I wasn't the friend I thought I was.

I watched her walk away, not saying a word. I watched her walk away, and I didn't do a thing to stop her. I felt like a stranger in her life, in our life, and in our friendship. A stranger to myself.

How did I not see what she felt for me? How did I not notice her discomfort, her pain? How did I not read her silences, her looks, the signs she must have been sending me?

I have so many questions spinning around in my head, colliding with each other like bouncing balls. I feel completely confused and so incredibly stupid. Stupid for not having answers to those questions, and stupid for even asking them.

It's been two days since I saw her last, and I haven't had the strength, or maybe the courage, to call her or even send a text. A heavy silence has settled between us, one I'm not used to. I'd always had this kind of symbiotic connection with her. A special bond. One of a kind. I only now realize that the moment Lorenzo entered my life, something shifted between us.

Right… Lorenzo. Eli's attitude changed the moment I started seeing him. Now, when I think about it, I remember those strange looks in her eyes, like she disapproved whenever I talked about him. Sometimes she'd shrug, leaving me feeling unsettled, because I knew she wasn't happy for me. She was putting up walls, building barriers of hostility and indifference between us. How dumb I was… For a while, I even thought she was jealous because I finally found a guy I really liked, while the only thing she had was that cyber world of hers, full of chats, usernames, and faces that would disappear into the nothingness of typed characters.

How could I have been so stupid?

And now her words echo in my mind: "When I think about losing you, it feels like the ground is caving in beneath my feet." Every letter is etched in my memory, every sound is burned into my mind. Her beautiful blue eyes staring at the floor: "I feel this sudden emptiness in my chest, this deafening noise in my head, like I'm losing my mind." Now I get it. Now I understand what she meant. Now that I too feel that emptiness, stronger than anything else. Now that it feels like I'm losing my mind, because I might have lost her forever.

Now I understand her fears.

ELIFE

Defendit numerus
There is safety in numbers
(Decimus Iunius Iuvenalis)

Numbers play a crucial role in my life, giving me a sense of peace and calm. They are something I can easily control and predict, unlike words. That's why I'm good at math. I owe it to them, the numbers. It's a kind of reward. Thanks to math, I, too, am someone in life and at school, and I've carved out a place for myself. Among my classmates, I stand out. I'm the best at math, the top of my class. Number one. There's probably no one as good as me in the entire school.

Everything has a number, a precise place in the universe, even though we often ignore the numbers we're assigned. My life is filled with numbers too. Sometimes, I even feel like they're haunting me. My mother was born on June 6, 1966: 6-6-66. My brother was born on August 8, 1988: 8-8-88. My father passed away on 01-02-2010, a so-called perfect date, a palindrome, because it reads the same forward and backward. Too bad for me, it's a day I'd rather forget. I was born on June 9: 6-9. I really like numbers 9 and 6 when they're together. They mirror each other. When I see them written on paper, they remind me of twins sleeping on white sheets, curled up in a fetal position, back to back, one upside down in bed. I like playing with numbers.

Balance and symmetry are two things I could never live without. Yes, I definitely like symmetry in the world around me, and I like my life to follow specific times and rhythms.

I wake up precisely at seven o'clock and have breakfast at seven-thirty. I brush my teeth for exactly two minutes, spending thirty seconds on each quadrant (upper right, upper left, bottom right, and bottom left). In the afternoon, I dedicate three hours to homework, splitting the time as evenly as possible between reading, reviewing, and reciting.

Five o'clock is tea time, which I have with five cookies. I only skip this ritual for Fiamma, when we're out shopping or walking in the park. At nine o'clock, I watch a movie in bed with my mom. Since my dad passed away, I've been sleeping next to her; we keep each other company at night. I like falling asleep to the sound of her breathing, it's steady, almost rhythmic. Sometimes, before bed, I read. I never read more than twenty-two pages a night and never less than three. I swam for eleven years. I studied violin for forty-four months. I sat through forty-four sessions with a therapist before quitting because I don't believe in therapy and never found it useful. I went on vacation with both my parents fourteen times, and after my dad's death, three times with just my mom.

I own eight pairs of shoes, six pairs of pants, two jackets, two vests, ten shirts, and ten sweaters. Lately, I've been wearing black pants and a white shirt. Black is the absence of color, or rather, it lacks all the colors that make up light. White contains every color in the electromagnetic spectrum; it's highly luminous but achromatic, meaning without hue. To me, together, they form the perfect balance.

I have three hundred and thirty-three Facebook friends. I stopped accepting requests at that number and won't take any new ones unless someone unfriends me. If that happens, I'll accept a new friend to keep the count at three hundred and thirty-three. I usually keep a few requests on standby just in case. Three hundred and thirty-three is an absolutely perfect number. Three times three. The perfect number repeated three times. Absolute perfection.

Of course, I don't actually have that many real friends. Most of those three hundred and thirty-three people are just profile pictures. I probably know no more than twenty of them personally. My only real friend is Fiamma.

The first time I saw her after school, I knew right away we could be special friends. She was impossible to miss, dressed like a steampunker. Funny thing was, I had just read about them a few days before. The article described steampunk as an artistic and cultural style depicting an alternate history, almost like a real-life utopia. The word is a combination of steam and punk, running parallel, or maybe in opposition, to cyberpunk. The biggest difference is that while cyberpunk is set in the future, steampunk looks to the past, particularly the Victorian era. The motto is: "What the past would look like if the future had happened sooner."

Put simply, a steampunk enthusiast is like a punk thrown into the Victorian Age, when steam was the cutting-edge technology.

I still remember what Fiamma wore that day: a skirt with a tail (a mini-skirt that was longer in the back), high lace-up boots, a brown corset over a white blouse, and a strange necklace made of a rubber cord holding a clock part. But the oddest part of her outfit was the top hat with a huge pair of goggles attached.

I remember thinking she was something else. Beautiful and strange at the same time. Out of place, like her clothes. Out of time and space, lost in her own universe. As far as I knew, no one else in our high school had ever dared to dress that way. And even though I love rules and order, I found her style absolutely captivating. Steampunk is the only illogical thing that fascinates me, though I could never dress that way myself.

Obviously, there's nothing practical about a movement whose slogan is "What the past would look like if the future had happened sooner." And yet, there's something irresistibly intriguing about the way Fiamma dresses.

I was the one who approached her. Even I was surprised, I have a hard enough time answering questions, let alone asking them. Embarrassed, I blurted out: "Cool goggles. Are you into steampunk?"

I went pale when she turned to look at me with vacant eyes. It was like I had woken her from a deep sleep, and part of her mind was still lost somewhere far away.

I felt so awkward, wishing I could sink into the ground, disappear into the generic clothes everyone else at school wore. But then Fiamma snapped out of it and smiled. And looking back, that smile was both my salvation and my downfall. All in one.

It wasn't an ordinary smile. A normal smile appears naturally, making whoever sees it feel at ease. Fiamma's smile was different, it belonged to someone who rarely smiled, who had forgotten how, or who hadn't smiled in a long time. It was the kind of smile that transforms a face, making it glow.

"Thanks! I made these goggles myself. It's actually not hard…a couple of screw-top jar lids, some rubber washers from a moka pot, leather cord, plastic bits…not much else. I found the instructions online. Of course I love steampunk! I love the clothes, the music…Abbey Park, Rasputina, and Emilie Autumn… What about you? Do you like it too? What kind of music do you listen to?"

Her voice felt oddly familiar, as if I had heard it a million times before, like it belonged in my world, meant to guide and comfort me. And yet I was sure I had never met this beautiful red-haired girl before.

I didn't disappoint her. I could hardly believe I was finally talking to someone who saw beyond appearances, who didn't care about my plain clothes or ordinary looks. I pretended to know the style. Luckily, I have an excellent memory and recalled a few bands mentioned in the article I'd read. Proudly, I answered:

"I like all the bands you do…plus The Clockwork Dolls. I love 'Blades in Autumn', you know, the song from their album *Dramatis Personae?*"

"Oh, yeah! I almost forgot about them," she gasped, covering her mouth as if she had made a huge mistake. "Blades in Autumn is one of my favorites! And you know what? Fall is my favorite season."

I told her I love fall too. And I wasn't lying. I really do. Maybe it's because of the way certain photographs look. Sepia, that's the color, if I'm not mistaken. A kind of reddish-brown. Red, like life, energy, action, and all the possibilities the future holds. Brown, like things that have already passed, ready to turn to dust, to fade into gray, to transform into something new, to slip away, knowing they've served their purpose.

My dad was born in October, in the heart of fall. And at the end of October 2009, on a cloudy day when fall was at its peak, sweeping away the last traces of summer and announcing the arrival of winter, we found out he had cancer. The worst kind. He didn't have more than four months left.

I remember the day he told us he had pancreatic cancer. He hugged me tightly, then looked into my eyes, gently touching my face. "It'll be alright, my little one," he said. "Be happy, always. And don't be afraid…"

In that moment, I understood how much he loved me. He was dying, yet all he cared about was me being happy, unafraid. My dad was the color red, the color of blood, of fire, of love. My memories of him are tinged with deep chestnut brown. And despite everything, fall remains my favorite season. It always will be.

My name is Fiamma, and lately, I find myself laughing at the irony of it. This ridiculous name you gave me, Dad. It fits me perfectly, almost in a cruel way.

My name is Fiamma. And everything around me, everything I touch, is destined to turn to ashes.

LORENZO

Barcelona is a soft carpet of dark alleyways, blackened by time. But no matter how maze-like, they feel strangely reassuring. And you start to think that maybe, in the end, getting lost in one of these narrow, winding streets wouldn't be so bad. Then you step into La Boqueria, where an explosion of colors surrounds you, leaving you frozen in place, overwhelmed. You stand there, counting the endless shades, realizing you're more disoriented now than you were before.

And then, suddenly, you're crying. Crying over a girl you thought was yours, who *was* yours just a second ago. Yours forever. Yours for this life and all the lives to come. You cry, but silently, not wanting to interrupt the joyful hum of voices spilling from the buildings around you. You cry, but in sync with the happiness that fills the air. It's a kind of joy that demands attention, so you listen, to the laughter, the chatter, between your quiet sobs.

From the narrow buildings lining La Rambla, threads of light spill down the ever-gray walls. Gray upon gray, beyond time, beyond memory.

Strange footsteps approach from around the bend.

It's not her.

It's not the girl you thought would be yours forever. Instead, it's a woman in a billowing skirt, a skirt that has grown fuller with the years, gathering time and memories in its fabric. She brushes past you. A group of tourists stops to take her picture, then she disappears into the distance, her footsteps echoing behind her. If you listen closely, you can hear her dreams, the ones she tramples underfoot as she wanders the streets, endlessly. If you stand still enough, you might even steal one, a dream flattened beneath her worn soles.

You wonder if she's ever felt the cold, trapped in the flashes of countless cameras, wrapped in her own madness, on display for eyes just like yours. But then, you let the thought go. Because this is just how the world turns. And there are too many mad people in it. Far too many.

So you light a cigarette, thinking it might warm the air around you. That maybe, for a moment, it will bring color to the gray alley stretching ahead. That maybe, just maybe, it will offer some kind of answer. A reason to keep going.

But as you watch the smoke curl into the air, you realize you were wrong. The gray remains, relentless. So you sink your hands into your pockets, searching for comfort. And there it is, a small piece of hope. The coins in your fingers still hold some warmth. Enough for a hot coffee. You wrap your jacket tighter around you and feel, for just a second, like a god. Because you can still afford a cup of coffee. And you lift your eyes.

They say Barcelona should be seen with your head tilted back.

It's the only way to take in the imperfect spires of the Sagrada Familia. The only way to appreciate the city's restless buildings, always shifting, never still.

So you walk like that. Even though your legs feel weak. Even though your heart feels weaker. Because she, the one you thought was yours, yours in this life and all the ones after, has taken something from you. Drained the life from your core.

And yet… for some reason… you keep walking.

You glance down and notice the hem of your jacket is torn. But you don't feel upset, don't even think to fix it. Instead, you hold onto the loose thread like an anchor. You roll it between your fingers, twirl it, flick it, watching it with your head lowered (weren't you supposed to be looking up?). You feel both embarrassed and oddly proud. And for a fleeting moment, you feel too close, *uncomfortably* close, to the woman with the billowing skirt, the one who has gathered years and memories in her wake.

You cough, not thinking much of it, until you feel something sharp and jagged in the back of your throat. And for a single, heavy second, your legs refuse to move. They feel rotten, useless, like they've suddenly grown roots, gripping the pavement, trapping you. You're sinking, as if invisible quicksand is pulling you under, draining the last of your strength.

And then, just a few feet away, you see a dog.

A scruffy thing, white but dirty, its fur sticking out in tufts. You laugh despite yourself. Something about the way he moves, his unsteady, delicate steps, like he's tiptoeing around imaginary puddles, lifts the weight pressing down on you.

His dark eyes are full of life. And somehow, that's enough.

So you follow him.

Your legs, your rotted limbs, come back to life. You take one shaky step. Then another. And another. And before you even realize it, you're moving forward. You don't know exactly where you're going, or why. But that doesn't matter.

You walk, your fingers still wrapped around the thread of your jacket, holding onto it like a lifeline. You walk with a new kind of respect, for the woman with the billowing skirt and for the little dog with his wobbly, determined gait.

And this time, you walk with your head held high.

Because from now on, you *will* see Barcelona with your eyes to the sky.

You walk toward the magnificent Sagrada Familia. Unfinished, but never incomplete. Just like life.

You walk slowly. But you don't stop. Not even for a second.

And as you go, you think of *her*, the one who, maybe (and this thought makes you smile, just a little), *maybe* will be yours one day.

Yours forever.

Yours for all the lives to come.

Some people are meant to stay in each other's lives forever.

That's the subject line of the email Fiamma just received from Elife. As she clicks on the message, her heart pounds. She's nervous, curious, hopeful, all at once. She holds her breath as she reads, re-reading each line as she goes.

> Some people are meant to stay in each other's lives forever, once they've found each other. They might drift apart, lose touch, live oceans apart or just a few feet away. They might go years without speaking. But they never really separate. They're connected by a thin thread, one that no one else can see, but they can.
> You and I are like that.
> Even if we ever stop seeing each other, even if we stop calling or writing, I don't think we could ever truly part.
> Maybe I never told you just how much you mean to me. How much you've meant to me this whole time. I know I'm not the kind of friend most people want. I'm not popular. I ramble about weird things or just say nothing at all.
> But you, you never made me feel like I had to be different. Most of all, I want to thank you for accepting my silences. There were a lot of them, and most of the time, they were my fault.

Because sometimes I don't know how to say what I'm feeling. Or maybe I don't think it's worth trying. Thank you for accepting this last, especially long silence. It gave me time to think, about us, about what happened the other day, about me. You know how much I love numbers. They make me feel safe, like I have control over things. For a long time, I thought I could control what I felt for you. That I could keep it hidden. But eventually, I realized I couldn't hide something so important from you. You have no idea how hard it was for me to say what I said the other day. But I'm glad I did. At least now, there are no more secrets between us.

When I think of us, I think of the number ten. I'm the zero. You're the one.

On our own, we don't add up to much, especially me. I've always been kind of a loser. But together? We make a perfect ten. Before I met you, I felt like a zero. A nobody. A freak.

I've always been the odd one out, the weird kid, the loner. Ever since I was little, people avoided me. Like they were afraid that if they got too close, they'd become invisible too. I got used to it, like it was something I just had to accept. Like there was no way to change it.

And then you showed up. My number One. And everything changed.

It's not like I'm suddenly popular or respected. But the way I feel, around other people, in life, in my own skin, it's different now.

The zero I used to be (or rather, the zero I felt like, the one people made me believe I was) took on a new meaning when we became friends.

And if I had to rate our friendship? It's a solid ten. No question.

Meeting you was the best thing that ever happened to me. And I don't want to lose you.

So… let's just pretend I never said what I said the other day, okay?

Well, not everything. Some of it, I meant. And I am glad I told you.

Like when I said I'll always be here for you. That's real. That's absolutely true. No matter what, no matter when. That will never change. Let's call that an absolute truth. But the rest? Maybe we can forget about that. Or at least… never talk about it again. I've always felt like I was on the edges of things. Like a footnote in a book, useful, but not essential. A tiny blot of black ink on a white page, there but easily ignored. Sometimes barely even noticed. You are the only person who has ever made me feel like I'm more than that. Like I could be more than that. You made me feel important, Fiamma. And I want to believe that I can stay important to you, for a long, long time.

See you tomorrow after school.

A hug,

Your favorite Zero.

There's a veil of joy in my sadness. A streak of yellow at the edge of a blank sheet of paper. My sadness is a question mark, dangling in the center of everything. It sits at the heart of my days, my thoughts, your absence, Dad, and Mom's broken presence.

Late at night, there's a strange sense of calm, something almost like happiness. The night that grants me sleep. The dogs howling, their cries bouncing off the walls. The faucet that releases one metallic drop after another. And the silence, snuffed out in the ashtray next to my last cigarette of the day.

Sometimes, I wish I could put out the thoughts crowding my head the same way I press this cigarette butt into the ashtray.

The sun is a pale disk of illusions, barely cutting through the thick gray sky on this early spring Sunday.

Fiamma is at the cemetery, visiting her father. She's brought him his favorite flowers, wildflowers, especially daisies. Daniel loved white daisies because he thought they were "naively beautiful." Fiamma remembers those words so well because he used them often. Every time he brought home a bunch of them, he'd say it with the excitement of a child.

"Look at them… aren't they lovely? So simple, so naively beautiful."

Fiamma loves daisies, too. As a child, she would draw them over and over, with huge yellow centers and countless white petals, thick and uneven, like little beams of light. She called them *ray flowers.*

Back then, she loved daisies but hated eggs. So her father came up with a solution: he cooked eggs in sun-shaped silicone molds. They didn't always turn out great, the yellow center was too big, the petals too small, and they often fell apart on the way from the pan to the plate. But she didn't care. Her father's daisy eggs were perfect.

She's placing the flowers in the vase next to his picture when her mother arrives.

Startled, Fiamma quickly runs through her memory, trying to figure out if today is some kind of anniversary, some special occasion for their family. But nothing comes to mind.

"Hey, hi!"

Her mother's voice is too loud. *Way* too loud,

considering where they are.

Fiamma sighs. Sometimes, her mother acts like a child, without filters, without limits. As if she's the only person in the world, and the world is just her stage.

Fiamma simply nods, offering a faint smile.

"You're here too, *amore*!" Sara nearly runs the last few steps to her daughter, stretching out the last syllable of the word.

Fiamma hates that word.

She counts in her head. Seven, maybe eight times she's heard her mother call her that. Including today. Definitely less than ten.

Again, she wonders if today is special. But nothing comes to mind.

So why *that* word?

Why use something that, coming from her, feels so vague and empty?

"Hey, Mom… what are you doing here?" Fiamma's voice is cautious, caught somewhere between surprise and annoyance.

"Well… probably the same reason you're here," Sara says, still smiling, cool and unbothered. "He loved daisies… Honestly, I never thought they were anything special. Too plain, too simple. But I've grown to appreciate them. Did you know daisies symbolize purity? And endless, patient love? I just read that the other day at the salon."

She pauses, looking at the flowers in Fiamma's hands.

"Your dad used to bring them to us all the time… do you remember? I read somewhere that giving someone daisies is a promise of eternal love and devotion. I think that's why he gave them to us. Don't you?"

Fiamma scoffs. "Wow. Impressive analysis. If this were

a class on the language of flowers, I'd give you an A+."

Her sarcasm wipes the smile off Sara's face instantly.

The enthusiasm she had just seconds ago, seeing her daughter standing by Daniel's grave, is gone.

For a split second, she wants to tell Fiamma she's being unfair. She wants to pull rank, demand a little respect, at *least* a little less hostility.

But then she remembers. She lost that right a long time ago.

Or maybe she never really had it.

So she says nothing.

Fiamma isn't even looking at her anymore. She's staring into space, already wishing she were somewhere else.

Anywhere but here.

Because her mother has a way of getting under her skin, of dragging reactions out of her, reactions she immediately regrets.

Sara has a way of making her feel guilty, even when she shouldn't.

Fiamma sighs.

"I was just kidding, you know…" Her voice is tired, like it belongs to someone else.

She glances at her mother and forces a small smile.

"Wanna buy me a cup of tea?"

*

She's nervous. She's always nervous around her mother.

She hates her. She loves her.

She doesn't understand her, and she can't make herself

understood. Or maybe she doesn't *want* to understand her. Maybe she doesn't *want* to be understood.

To Fiamma, Sara is perfect. Too perfect. So beautiful. So sophisticated. So polished, no matter where she is or who she's with. Always put together. Always elegant. Always poised.

Always *flawless*.

When Fiamma looks at Sara, she doesn't see a mother. She just sees *Sara*.

What she *doesn't* see is how out of place Sara feels, how insecure she is, *all* the time. Not just with her daughter, but everywhere. Though she'd never show it.

Fiamma doesn't know that before her mother walks out the door, she checks her hair in the mirror at least a hundred times. That she only relaxes when she catches at least a hundred approving glances. She doesn't know that her mother is at war with the calendar and the scale. That every morning comes with a small, sharp panic, another gray hair, another wrinkle. That she spends hours at the gym, forcing herself forward, one more mile, one more rep, trying to burn off the glass of prosecco and the cake she *should* have refused.

There are so many things Fiamma doesn't know about her mother.

Like the fact that things with Giorgio have been bad for a while. *A long while.*

Months.

The café is as dreary as the cemetery across the street. White plastic chairs. Dull gray walls. The kind of place where time slows down, where voices seem to carry a little too far.

Sara stirs her drink, watching the spoon swirl through the thick liquid. She usually orders pineapple juice. But today, she's drinking hot chocolate.

Fiamma notices. And though she doesn't say anything, she feels the slightest hint of satisfaction.

"I'm thinking about leaving him," Sara says.

The spoon clinks against the porcelain cup.

"I don't think I ever really loved him," she continues after a pause. "Maybe I was just… grateful. Grateful that he gave me a job, a nice home…" She exhales, looking almost embarrassed. "The truth is, Daniel was the only man I ever really loved."

She hesitates, as if she regrets saying it. As if she wishes she could take it back.

The look on Fiamma's face doesn't help.

"Yes," Sara says again, this time with more certainty. "I think, no, I *know*, that in my entire life, I've only ever loved one man. Your father."

Fiamma's chest tightens.

"So why did you move in with him?!" she bursts out, louder than she meant to.

The bartender, wiping down glasses, pauses. His eyes flick toward them, one brow raised.

Fiamma lowers her voice, but it's firm. Unyielding.

"I don't get it," she says. "Why the hell did you move in with that bastard? And why did you stay for so long if you didn't even love him?"

She wants answers. *Needs* them.

Answers that will explain why they both had to suffer for *years*.

Because for as long as she can remember, Fiamma has believed she was the sacrifice. That her mother traded her happiness, *her well-being*, for a life with Giorgio.

But now?

Now she finds out Sara was *never* happy. Not

completely. *Not even for a moment.*

And that feels like betrayal.

Another betrayal.

One more disappointment, too massive to bear.

Unacceptable.

As unacceptable as her mother's silence.

Sara just stares into the distance, swirling her spoon in what's now only cold chocolate.

"Mamma, answer me."

Fiamma's voice is sharp. Desperate.

She's *begging* for an explanation, with her words, with her eyes.

Sara sighs.

"Don't ask, *amore*…"

There it is. *That damn word.*

Twice in one day. Maybe eight, nine, ten times total in her life.

If this weren't such a moment, Fiamma would tell her to stop using it. Because it *bothers* her. *Because it's empty.*

But right now, she doesn't care.

Right now, she just wants answers.

"Don't ask me," Sara says again, voice low. "I wouldn't even know what to tell you…"

Fiamma says nothing.

Sara exhales slowly.

"When I think about your father's illness, about the time after his death… all I see is black. Like the curtain falling after a show. And beyond that? *Nothing.* No past, no future. It was like life just stopped, frozen in a time and place that didn't exist anymore. And I was there, waiting for something I *knew* would never come."

She pauses.

"You ask why I moved in with Giorgio? *Everyone* asked

me that. I asked myself that. Over and over. And I never found an answer. So eventually, I stopped asking. Instead, I asked myself something else. Something completely different."

Sara looks up, finally meeting Fiamma's eyes.

"If I could go back… knowing what I know now. Knowing that Daniel would get sick. That he would suffer. That nothing could be done to stop it.

Would I still choose him?

Would I still choose him to be my partner? To be the father of my child?

Even knowing I'd have to lose him?"

A beat.

Then she nods.

"Yes," she says. "Yes. A million times, yes. Just *yes*."

Her head tilts forward slightly, as if she's sinking into the steam rising from her cup. For a second, it almost seems like she might disappear.

When she lifts her face again, her eyes glisten.

"The love I had for your father, the love I *still* have for him, is the only thing I'm certain of. That, and my love for you. He was *it* for me. The love of my life."

She blinks, shaking her head.

"And instead of feeling unlucky for losing him… I feel *lucky* that I had him. That I got to love him at all. Because I was happier with him than I ever deserved to be. And happier than most people will *ever* be in their entire lives."

Sara's voice falters.

"So you can imagine how devastating it was to lose him. Actually, no. *Devastating* isn't the right word. But there *is* no right word. No adjective strong enough to describe that kind of pain."

She looks down, as if gathering herself.

"There's only one 'love of your life.' That's why they call it that. And when I lost Daniel, I knew, *knew*, that no one else could ever compare. So… I settled.

Giorgio was just a placeholder. A warm body to take up space in the emptiness."

She meets Fiamma's gaze again.

"And that answers your first question.

As for the second… why I stayed so long?"

She exhales.

"Because sometimes it's easier to just *watch* yourself live than to actually *live*. It's easier to let things happen to you than to ask yourself if there's something better. It takes less energy.

And I was weak.

I *am* weak."

Another pause. This time, Sara pushes the cup of chocolate away and looks Fiamma in the eyes.

"But I don't have to tell you that. You're smart. You've always been smart. Smarter than other kids your age. You *know* I'm weak. We *both* know it. What I *don't* know…"

She hesitates.

"…is just *how* weak a mother has to be to lose sight of her own daughter's well-being."

A pause. A breath.

"But maybe one day, you'll tell me."

She takes the subway to go visit Blue. She woke up this morning with a powerful urge to see her and talk to her. But really, just seeing her would be enough. Sharing in her silence, in the way she smokes those hand-rolled cigarettes, just paper and tobacco, no filter. Fiamma has always been fascinated by her skill, how easily and quickly she rolls them, wrapping those tiny leaves in delicate paper with her fingertips, like a skilled pianist: tuck, roll, lick, and seal. Once her creation is done, Blue inhales deeply, furrowing her brow and hollowing her already sunken cheeks. She holds the smoke in, shuts her eyes, moves her lips like she's savoring fine wine, then exhales a gray cloud that vanishes into the stale air surrounding her and this part of the city. Fiamma has come to appreciate this whole ritual, every breath of death, every rank smell that clings to her strange friend like a second skin. She's grown to love it, just as she has grown to love her silences and blunt responses, her raw and brutally honest opinions. Yes, because Blue is like her cigarettes: unfiltered when she speaks to Fiamma or anyone else, and she couldn't care less. To most people, she's just another crazy lady.

But to Fiamma, Blue is someone whose suffering has given her clarity and the strength to detach from the judgment of others. Every time Fiamma greets her, offering the usual bottle of beer from the nearby coffee shop along with a simple "hi," she feels a bit foolish. As always, Blue simply nods with cool detachment, as if to say, "Oh, it's you again. I expected you, but that doesn't mean I need you or anything..." Today is no different.

After the hello, the beer, and the muttered thanks, Fiamma sits down on the grimy storefront steps beside Blue's wheelchair and starts unloading her latest updates. She talks about Lorenzo, about what went down with Elife, and with her mom. Her words pour out, coaxed by Blue's reliable, composed silence. Sometimes she stumbles, gets tangled up in her own thoughts, and has to circle back. She recaps everything she's been through these past few days, her hopes, her disappointments, and her fears. Love. And when she finishes, she lets out a long sigh, like she's trying to push out all the uncertainty and doubt inside her. She glances at her friend, who has been listening quietly, her gaze fixed on the coffee shop entrance, and for the first time, that silence becomes heavy. Blue's silence is hard to handle, so Fiamma fills the space with more words:

"I had to come be with you today, away from everything else. I don't even know why. Maybe it's because the past few days have just... sucked. It's hard to explain. Lonely days, definitely. Lonely and unsettling. I really needed a friend to guide me, to help me figure out which path to take. I guess I still need that. Probably always will. But more than that... I don't know... I have this ache in my chest, this dull but deafening pain. I haven't been feeling well, worse than usual, and I don't know how to handle it or where to go with it. That's all."

Words spilling out after she's mulled them over, just like when she binges on food. That's how Fiamma sees it. A terrible burden lifted, exhaled in a puff of gray smoke that drifts off into the air with the stench of Blue's tobacco. She realizes she now feels even dumber than when she first sat down. But also more alive than ever.

Blue stays quiet for a while, sipping her beer and smoking. Then suddenly, she speaks.

"Whenever I think about young people today, I remember this quote I read once about Lightness. I can't recall it word for word, so I can't quote it exactly, but the idea was that you have to let some lightness into your life sometimes. And by lightness, it doesn't mean being shallow. It means giving yourself permission to float, now and then. Float with your heart, your thoughts, just float. I think there's real truth in that. Lightness should be part of youth, one of its defining features. But what I see in the eyes of young people I meet, or pass by, is loneliness, disappointment, and a lack of light. And especially a lack of Lightness."

She emphasizes the last word, pausing, then blowing out a puff of smoke, her eyes lifting to the sky, then closing. She continues:

"Try not to be like everybody else, if you can help it. Don't take the well-worn route if you know it leads nowhere. Don't take any route unless you're sure it takes you where *you* really want to go. Try blazing your own trail, even if it's not on any map. Sure, it might be risky. You might get lost. But that doesn't mean it's the wrong way. Either way, it'll be your way.

"Follow it, explore it. Take in the scenery. And if, at some point, you realize it leads nowhere, if it turns out to be a rotten path, you can always turn back and start again.

"But if you go down a road everyone else has already taken, you'll know exactly where it ends, and you'll also know you left behind a thousand other possibilities that no one dared explore. When you walk, look straight ahead. Enjoy the trip. And always keep a spark in your eyes, the spark of someone who's out to discover something new, something better, something truly beautiful."

For the first time since they met, Blue looks Fiamma in

the eye. Then she adds:

"You said you don't know how to handle the pain you're carrying. Well, you don't have to *handle* it. Not always. Sometimes, you just need to *listen* to it, especially if it's as deafening as you say. Instead of trying to break free from it, sit with it. Listen to what it's trying to tell you. Sometimes the answers come exactly like that: through stillness, and silence."

Blue notices that Fiamma can't maintain eye contact anymore. She's looking around: at the filthy steps, the wheelchair, the café, the people walking by. Blue watches her sad face carefully, and what she sees reminds her of a girl she once knew long ago.

She looks away, shuts her eyes, and keeps speaking:

"Don't make the same mistake I did. Never lose yourself because of someone else. Don't hand over your life or your happiness to anyone. You're not stupid, just overly sensitive, like I used to be. Walk your own path, and you'll find that with every step, your legs get stronger, and not just your legs. They'll carry you wherever you want to go, all on your own. Stop pitying yourself and expecting others to hand you happiness. You have to find it yourself, inside yourself, not out there."

Fiamma stays quiet. She's trying to make sense of her thoughts. Then she asks:

"What if I realize I *had* happiness and lost it? Or... what if I know there's someone who can make me happy, happier than I've felt in a long time, and just the thought of losing them makes me feel like I'm sinking, like I'm drowning?"

Now it's Blue's turn to fall silent. She stops smoking and stares at the tiny cigarette butt in her hand.

"If you really, truly believe that person brought you

happiness..." she says after a pause. "Then do everything you can to keep them close. Because if you don't, you'll regret it for the rest of your life."

A pause. Blue draws on the already finished cigarette until it practically vanishes between her lips.

"Let me say this again: don't give up who you are for anyone. Never lose sight of yourself, and don't let anyone else control your life or your happiness. That's on you," she finishes, staring blankly into the distance. "Now go. Leave this worn-out old woman and this miserable place. Go live your life. Get off this dirty stoop and start your journey. There are already too many sad, lonely, broken people in the world."

Fiamma gives her a small smile, then stands up without saying a word. She nods, just like Blue always does, a thank you without words. The nod says it all: "I understand. Thank you. No need to say more."

She walks into the coffee shop, buys a beer and a pouch of tobacco for Blue. When she finally leaves, she simply smiles at her friend. She expects Blue to return the smile, but instead, she surprises her. Blue meets her gaze and whispers:

"Thank you. For everything. For being here, for your words. But most of all, thank you for the silence we shared. That meant a lot to me."

Fiamma replays those words again and again in her head as she heads to the subway. She's overwhelmed by mixed feelings: happiness for having helped someone and having it acknowledged, and a deep, unexplained sadness. So deep her eyes well up.

When the train arrives, its metal bulk punches the air inside the narrow tunnel, packed with people. Fiamma is jolted out of her daze and hit with a wave of foul smells:

sweat, grime, rage, and loneliness. She closes her eyes, like doing so might shut out the chaos and filth around her. She remembers that her friend Blue smelled like something good. A scent she had come to recognize and cherish, one that didn't scare her, because it was familiar. And because, despite everything, it didn't carry rage or loneliness.

*

Fiamma had just finished brewing a cup of coffee when she caught the headline on a local news site:

Tragedy at the station: A disabled homeless woman struck by a high-speed train. Early reports suggest suicide.

The sound of her spoon clinking against the ceramic mug seemed to slice through the silence like glass splintering in slow motion. Fiamma's hand froze mid-air, holding nothing, while her heart missed a beat before slamming back into rhythm with doubled intensity. A sharp, knotted feeling gripped her stomach. She wanted to believe she was wrong, but deep inside, she already knew. She *knew*.

It was Blue. It was Blue. It was Blue.

Three words. Looping in her head like a broken record.

When she gets to the station, and then to the little café, there's no sign of her. No wheelchair. No vibrant, overflowing bags. No Blue.

She walks into the café, its doors just now yawning open to swallow the sleepy hum of early morning patrons. The same weathered tables. The familiar smell of roasted beans. The usual shuffle of tired customers. Everything is exactly as it should be, except her. Blue is gone.

She's flown away on her own broken wings. She's chased after one last train, just like she did once before, chasing after the lover who abandoned her. But this time, she didn't look back. No goodbye. No warning. She took her odd wisdom, her cryptic sentences, her worn-out magic, and her funny little blue hat, and vanished.

Fiamma doesn't know whether to laugh or collapse. For a second, she teeters between the two. Should she be grateful that Blue is finally free? Or devastated to have one less person in her corner? In the end, grief wins. Her body caves under the weight of it. She cries. Real tears, the kind she hasn't shed in ages. She sobs as strangers file in and out of the café, heading toward trains and destinations she no longer cares about. She stares at the empty spot where Blue used to sit, the one square meter of the world that had become her anchor.

And in her mourning, Fiamma becomes more acutely aware of her own body than she's ever been. She feels her pulse pounding in her chest, her tears streaking down her face, sweat trailing along her spine, and the tight pinch of her bra strap digging into her skin. It's all heightened, every sense, every sensation. As though brushing up against Death has sharpened her awareness of Life.

No one stops to ask if she's okay. No one pauses to check in. Not one person acknowledges the girl crying in plain sight. Blue would've said, *"People don't have time to value Time anymore."*

And maybe that's for the best, Fiamma thinks. Maybe it's better to let this place stay what it is: a crowded, soulless stop full of blurred faces in a constant rush from nowhere to nowhere. Maybe it's a kind of peace to know that Blue is far from all of it now, far from this noisy, dirty world where she was trapped in a wheelchair, surrounded by plastic bags stuffed with memories.

Fiamma doesn't know if she believes in God, but she likes the image of Blue sharing a good bottle of wine with Him, floating comfortably on a soft white cloud.

Maybe, in the end, it really *is* better this way.

She's running now. No real direction. Just sprinting like someone lost, or like a kid who doesn't care how ridiculous they look, running in messy circles on an invisible playground. Her chest is tight, her breathing ragged, her legs burning, but she doesn't stop. She can't. She won't.

Because stopping might mean giving in. Stopping might mean disappearing, like Blue.

Her Blue. Blue, who left her behind without even letting her say goodbye. Another person gone. Another betrayal.

She passes a couple of tourists, maybe in their fifties, hauling oversized backpacks. The man looks like he's in pain, and the woman wears a wide-eyed, innocent expression, as if everything around her is brand new. He's soaked in sweat. She's marveling at the world like a child. For a second, Fiamma cracks a smile. They look like giant tortoises, two tired teenagers who suddenly woke up middle-aged, as if in a strange, slow-motion dream. They waddle away with their burdens.

Up ahead, she spots a teenager dressed in all black, his cap pulled low. He's tagging a rundown wall with spray paint. She watches his hand rise, trembling, painting the word **HOPE** in bold, red letters. He shakes the can after each one, and then, just like that, he bolts.

Fiamma feels a sudden impulse to chase after him. To run with him, away from the weight, away from the ache. Just disappear. Not forever, just long enough to forget. Or to remember something better.

That old quote flashes in her mind: *"It only takes a moment to recognize someone special, and a lifetime to forget them."* She thinks about how some people walk into your life and pierce it without warning. Like a thumbtack through soft cork. Leaving holes. Real ones. Deep and wide as craters. Craters that never close up.

For Fiamma, Blue was one of them.

There are people who stumble into this world by accident. Maybe you were never really meant to stay, Dad. Maybe you were just an angel passing through.

And maybe Blue was, too.

I wish I could go back. Back to when I was full of life and hope, the way I used to be. I want to be that little girl again, the one who believed anything was possible if she just wished hard enough. I used to think fireflies were pieces of stars that had fallen to Earth, ripe and ready to be picked like fruit.

I remember chasing them like mad in the countryside at my aunt's house. Jar in one hand, lid in the other, laughing and running after those glowing specks while you cheered me on, Dad, daring me to catch just one.

I never did.

Not a single damn firefly.

But now? Now I want to try and catch the tiny flickers of light you left behind in my life. That's why I'm lighting up each memory of you, one by one, and tucking them into this page, like little coins of light.

That's why I've decided to try something different.

To be happy. Or at least to try to be happy. So that wherever you are now, you might look down and see me smiling, doing my best to be a little like you.

That's why I'm putting my pride, my fear, my shame aside.

That's why I'm writing to Lorenzo.

From: fiamma.burgagni@gmail.com
To: lore.ebano@yahoo.it

I haven't heard from you. And I know there's no real reason to keep waiting, to go looking for you, or to search for something in you that might hold us together. You're like the echo of a memory, fading in and out, like the thick haze of a dream when I wake up. What exactly held us close before you left? Was it the way we looked at each other? The emails, the texts, the words? The body heat? And of course, let's not forget the tangle of emotions, just sprinkles on a half-baked cake.

And now…

Now you're moving through this world without me. Your skin brushing against millions of dust particles. Strangers' eyes landing on your face, the one I loved, the one I touched. Others will touch you now, kiss you, and I won't know a thing about it. You'll walk down streets I've never heard of, through cities whose names mean nothing to me. Maybe you'll sit in a café somewhere and sip a coffee, while I'm miles away, sleeping…maybe dreaming of you. You'll be on the move, stopping to rest here and there, and maybe, just maybe, before you close your eyes, you'll think of us. Maybe you'll miss me. Maybe you'll wish to come back. You'll fall asleep remembering how we used to be, wondering if the touch on your cheek was just a dream, a longing, or a memory of something real, something we lost. You'll wake up, and I won't be next to you. But I'll still be somewhere, alive, unchanged, just as you last saw me.

The image of me saying goodbye, that face, will follow you wherever you go. In every unknown place you visit, in every undiscovered corner of the world.
That version of me will stay frozen in time. Always under the same sky. Familiar but changed. And maybe it'll speak to you of me. Maybe.

From: lore.ebano@yahoo.it
To: fiamma.burgagni@gmail.com

I'm sorry I didn't write sooner.
I kept trying to find the right words. I didn't want to say something cliché. But every time I started, everything I typed just sounded flat.
I guess I should apologize.
Sorry for walking away. For hurting you. Sorry even for the good memories, because I know they'll sting more than anything else. That's the worst part, isn't it? Happy memories that become painful because they're gone. Because they're never coming back.
But instead of just saying I'm sorry, I owe you an explanation. So here it is.
I left because, lately, that's what I do. I want you to know, I wasn't running from you. I was running from what I felt when I was with you.
The feelings were too intense. And I'm not good with feelings like that. Call me a coward, or an asshole, if you want. Say whatever you need to, but don't ever think I left because something was wrong with you, or with us, or what we had.
Because what we had, what we have, was the one true, beautiful thing in my life. I mean that.
And every mile I put between us just reminds me of how much you mean to me. No amount of dust can cover the memory of your touch. Just like tonight, I fall asleep thinking about us, what we were, what we could've been.

199

You'll always be here when I wake up, in my thoughts, curled up in the back of my heart.

Just like that last night, when I pretended to be asleep, but was really just listening to your breath.

Say what you will about me, but I never lied to you. And I really did love you. I just... didn't have the strength to keep living something so huge. Too big. For me. For who I am right now.

But your smile, your hands on me, those things won't fade. I promise. That memory will always be with me. No maybes.

From: fiamma.burgagni@gmail.com
To: lore.ebano@yahoo.it

You're talented with words, I'll give you that. Just as skilled as you are with your bottles. Every syllable settles at the bottom of your glass soldiers, safe in the knowledge they won't betray you. You trust that no note will break rank. Nothing will challenge the neat little order your fingers create as they dance across that hollow world of sounds. But here's the thing: love needs something real. True love doesn't live off words floating midair or rippling on the surface of uncertainty, waiting for direction. Sometimes, all love really needs is a single *Do* and *La*, two notes, nothing more. Just a touch that says, "I'm here. Right now. And I'm not going anywhere."

From: lore.ebano@yahoo.it
To: fiamma.burgagni@gmail.com

Love needs something real, you say... and you're right. You totally are.

That's actually why I left. Because I know I can't give you the kind of solid love you deserve, something more than just words drifting in air.

To me, love's like a tattoo: beautiful on someone else, but on me... I'm scared. It's permanent. And permanence... well, it just doesn't feel poetic to me.

From: fiamma.burgagni@gmail.com
To: lore.ebano@yahoo.it

Sure. You're probably right.
If you believe that anything permanent lacks poetry, then maybe you also think anything without poetry has no reason to exist.
So the logic goes: love is permanent, therefore it lacks poetry... and so love has no purpose. End of story, right?

From: lore.ebano@yahoo.it
To: fiamma.burgagni@gmail.com

I'm not big on logic, but I do know one thing: I might be good with words, like you said, but I'm no poet. And I'm definitely not built to handle a love as poetic as yours.
To me, love feels like the dampness of a goodbye, like a soggy heart you could squeeze in your palm like a sponge. It's a memory tinged with sepia, something from the past, stuck in your head.
I wish I could say something like: "Let's build winter castles together, castles with drawbridges we'd raise to keep out the loud, colorless joy of the world."
I wish I could tell you we'd drink the snow from white sand dunes when pain burns our lips. I wish I could flood you with words full of hope, beauty, and poetry.
I wish I could. Truly. But the only love I have to give right now feels sick inside me. Behind the quickened pulse and the burst of spring scents, there's something rotten. Me. I'm what's rotten. I don't know how to love.

201

From: lore.ebano@yahoo.it
To: fiamma.burgagni@gmail.com

It's three in the morning. Or three at night. Depends how you see it.
I'm writing again now, while the night fades and day begins to peek in.
Maybe because you're asleep. Maybe because I hope you won't read this right away. It makes the words feel lighter. Less embarrassing.
We do strange things when we think no one's looking…
I'm sending you a poem I wrote a while ago. I was thinking about my dad, and how he went from being the perfect husband, sober, handing my mom armfuls of roses, to a full-on monster.

quilts and thorns
by L.E.

the rose
that grazes the wood table
in the dining room
points toward plaster walls
that pretend not to hear
beneath bricks that refuse to speak.
she left it there, vase-less,
after he placed it in her hand,
still bruised.
the rose, silent,
a passive witness,
alibi with no story
for another night of caged dreams.
he throws her on a bed of quilts and thorns.
he strokes each bruise

with fingers made of petals.
and she lets him pick her, again,
always in silence.
and as the final root snaps,
she thinks, bitterly,
of rose thorns,
unyielding,
like tiny, proud nipples
suckled forever
by sleeping children.

I don't know why I'm sharing this. Maybe I just needed an excuse to say how ridiculous I feel. Yeah. Ridiculous.
I feel like a pile of skin and bones, hobbling through life. A half-man, floating in a void.
Just... ridiculous.

From: fiamma.burgagni@gmail.com
To: lore.ebano@yahoo.it

If only you would trust me...
If only you'd let me... I'd take you far from all this. I don't know where exactly. But maybe I could help you see the world differently. Maybe we could unravel some knots.
If you'd let me, we could laugh away the fear and the weight of time.
You don't see it, but I'm here. I'm trying to look past your fog, through mine.
Trying to see you. Trying to let you see us.
If you'd let me, maybe tonight would just be tonight, not an eternity.
If you let me through that tiny crack you've left open, God knows why, maybe we could run.
Run together.

I've learned not to measure love by how long it lasts, but how deeply it lives.

And if you think love is a tattoo, I think it's an embrace, one that sticks to your skin, invisible and endless.

Can you feel it? What lingers on us, in silence?

If you let me, I'd take you back to those days when we made love without saying a word. And then, wordless, I'd pull you away with just a gesture, or a lie said gently if needed.

I'd carry you far, from our skin, our fear, our hands.

Do you feel me? I'm here. I'm not leaving. I can't take a single step without you beside me.

So I create you. Over and over again. Since the day you left.

I make you up. And I take you with me. Far from here. Far from everything.

From: lore.ebano@yahoo.it
To: fiamma.burgagni@gmail.com

When dusk falls over this city, it swallows everything in soft melancholy. The red light melts over rooftops, silencing sound. It's a suspended kind of quiet.

There's this hour when Barcelona just... dozes.

It breathes again only once the night comes.

It's fleeting, but magical.

You walk around wondering where the voices went, why the noise vanished.

Then, boom, you turn a corner, and there it is again: laughter, shouts. Night is here.

The final slivers of daylight disappear. And with them, you're pulled back into the living city, a city that never sleeps, always in motion, ready to welcome you or let you go.

Barcelona at night isn't for everyone.

You might pass a girl in scarlet boots, or an older

woman with orange hair who doesn't smile.
Or that old guy in the Brazil jersey, I've seen him three times now! I think he's following me...
He's not Brazilian. He just said a kid gave him the shirt one night, long ago.
Anyway, like I said, Barcelona at night isn't for everyone. But everyone should see it once.
It's got every color, every emotion, from the simplest blue to deep violet.
It's a living rainbow of feelings.
I love it because it makes me feel close to my mom.
She was Spanish. Born in a little town nearby. She used to tell me about this road in Barcelona lined with flowers that led to the sea.
She always said we'd walk it together one day.
I haven't found that road yet.
Maybe I'm not looking the right way.
But if you were here with me now, this whole city would shine brighter.
It would feel complete.
Maybe one day I'll find that road. And maybe, just maybe, we'll pick flowers together.

From: fiamma.burgagni@gmail.com
To: lore.ebano@yahoo.it

Barcelona again, huh?
How long are you staying there? You said you never stick around one place too long...
Also, you didn't even mention my last email. Are you dodging it?
Anyway, I liked the flower-lined road story.
Maybe in another lifetime, or in some far-off future, we'll walk it together.
I'm feeling sarcastic today. Or maybe I just want to make you feel guilty. Sure, I bet Barcelona is lovely, but Rome?

Rome is Rome. The heart of the world. History's cradle.
The streets here may not bloom with petals, but they're thick with memories. And maybe, just maybe, they'll help me forget you.
Just like everything else we've forgotten.

*

She regretted sending that last email the second she hit *Send.* And she regretted it even more when Lorenzo didn't write back. His silence weighs on her like a stone, and the hours crawl by. Not knowing where he is, what he's thinking, who he's with, or what he's doing makes her feel helpless. She's sure she was too harsh, too sarcastic. How could she have said those things? Who does she think she is? What gave her the right to be so smug, so self-righteous? She wishes she could rewind time, take it all back, delete every word. She hopes he doesn't even read it, because it wasn't what she meant to say.

So this time, she chooses something simpler. A text. Short, direct… but honest.

I miss you. I miss you and feel hollow without you. Like a locked chest in the dark, heavy with a strange curiosity and a surprising emptiness. The memory of your touch slips through my fingers; the scent of your skin falls from my lips like a cascade of kisses. If I stay quiet, I can still hear your voice in my head.

From: lore.ebano@yahoo.it
To: fiamma.burgagni@gmail.com

I feel hollow too. And I miss you.
I didn't like reading certain parts, not the sarcasm, but the last few lines. They cut deep. But I get where you're coming from. I really do. Even if it hurts, I can't blame you.
Right now, I don't have much to say. I'd rather stay quiet.
I just want to close my eyes… and find you inside me. Maybe, if you want, you could do the same. Close your eyes, and look for me.

From: fiamma.burgagni@gmail.com
To: lore.ebano@yahoo.it

I did what you said. I closed my eyes, and I looked for you.
And I found you, right there, in the first moment our hands brushed. It felt just like that first time.
I remember it so clearly. It was like a jolt, like electricity, but the charge came from somewhere deep inside me, and from so far away. So much time has passed since then, and yet, when I close my eyes, I still feel that sudden shock, that wild surge of energy rushing through my veins, oxygen in every cell.
Another day has gone by without you.
I claw at time's surface with my fingertips, dragging myself forward, reaching for you. I try to touch your skin, to caress your thoughts. I try to speak, but the words won't come. My fingers hover uselessly above the keyboard. I stare out into this uncertain spring, at a bare sun stripped of its light. And I miss you more than in a thousand moonlit nights. Because in this tiny fragment of day, I know you're not here. Not in

my bed. And I don't know if you'll show up in my dreams.

That's when I feel the most foolish. The most fragile. I fall asleep thinking of you, but without feeling you near. And without knowing where you are, physically or emotionally.

From: lore.ebano@yahoo.it
To: fiamma.burgagni@gmail.com

I'm here now. I'm always here. Especially in that moment before you fall asleep.

I hold you, without touching you, as you drift off, even if you can't see me.

Let me wrap you in silence. Let me hum you a lullaby in a language you don't understand, while your breath grows slower, deeper.

Can't you feel me there? I've never really left.

Can you hear the sea inside my mind?

The waves rise and fall on the shore, just like your chest as you sleep. I place two seashells over your ears and shut out the world. I build a wall between you and everything else, so all you can hear is the thunder of my silent gaze.

I watch you sleep. Your lips move gently, like fish beneath the surface, soft, wordless kisses, maybe meant for me.

I brush my mouth over yours, leaving behind a salty trace, ocean and tears. Your body stirs ever so slightly, almost imperceptibly, but you don't wake.

You lie on your side, perfectly still. A cliff I climb with fingers, with hands. My nails tickle, move like a crab's legs.

If you were awake, you'd swat me away. Or you'd laugh and run.

But you're asleep now. Breathing so slowly it feels like it might stop at any moment.

209

The sea of my desire follows your rhythm.
The waves rise, and fall, even slower. They stretch across two shores, two pieces of time, leaving behind an infinite space of emptiness and fullness.
I hold you in my arms without touching you. And I fall asleep, too, next to you, smiling.

As she walks down the stairs of her apartment building, taking the trash out, Fiamma has no idea what this rainy day is about to bring her.

The sky is a heavy, gray dome, more winter than spring, and definitely not the summer that's supposed to be around the corner.

To Fiamma, it's just another Sunday afternoon.

The clink of dishes carries from other apartments, and the air is rich with the smell of food. There's that special hush of full bellies, broken only by random laughter and the distant hum of a motorcycle.

But what she doesn't know is that Lorenzo is standing outside, trying to find the courage to press the buzzer. Or even just send a text.

He's just spent ten hours riding his motorcycle to get here. Battling sleep, muscle aches, numb fingers gripping the handlebars.

Lorenzo, who, the moment he arrives, suddenly feels every pound of the world settle on his shoulders, as if he's aged fifty years.

Lorenzo, who, just now, as he sees her descending the stairs in a sweatshirt covered in a hundred kittens, wearing pom-pom slippers and a mess of hair, feels brand new again. Like he just woke up from the best sleep of his life.

Through the glass door, his eyes say it all: hello, I missed you, I love you, and this time, I'm not going anywhere.

When she spots him, wrinkled jeans, stained white T-shirt, massive backpack at his feet, she can't believe what she's seeing. She squints, like she's nearsighted, like she needs to bring him into focus, though she sees him just fine. She holds the door open, trash bag dangling like a forgotten doll.

"What are you doing here?" she manages to say, voice trembling, eyes wide.

Lorenzo just smiles. He's decided he wants that smile to stay on his face forever, like a tattoo.

He only says three words: I am back.

Three words. So simple. Yet for Fiamma, they stretch across time and space, intersecting at infinity.

I'm back.

And those words alone would've been enough to light up her whole world. But Lorenzo doesn't stop.

"I'm here to stay. I rode all this way for you. I'm beyond exhausted, but it'd be worse to keep drifting around with no purpose. And without you.

I've always been on the move, never putting down roots. I wasn't traveling. I was running.

Always thinking about the next place, never appreciating where I was."

And just like that, the rain stops.

Maybe only in her mind, but that's all that matters.

"I don't know what I'm going to do here. Honestly, I don't even know if you want me here.

And if you don't…I don't know what I'll do. I don't know how we'll make it work. But I'm here now. And I'm not going anywhere."

Lorenzo's words are a rainbow.

No matter what the weather's doing, they're every color all at once.

They're green, like spring leaves and life and hope. Blue, like water, sky, dreams. Yellow, like sunlight, laughter, joy.

I'm back. I'm here to stay.

When Lorenzo speaks, he pulls Fiamma into a world of orange light. Orange like ripe fruit, like warmth, like something sweet you didn't expect.

Red pours from his lips like fire, like roses, like blood pumping hot and fast.

She listens, a candle flickering in a quiet church, wrapped in purple, solemn, steady, open.

And she follows him, wordlessly, into his eyes, where cyan and magenta melt into the darkest indigo.

Outside, the sun might be hidden behind thick clouds.

But to Fiamma, it's already shining.

ASHES

> *Post fata resurgo.*
> *After death, I will rise again.*
> *(Motto of the Phoenix)*

> Ashes have all kinds of uses:
> they can be used to make soap,
> cook food, melt ice on roads, fertilize soil,
> degrease surfaces, polish steel and silverware,
> and even remove water rings from wooden furniture.
> *(Folk wisdom)*

She and Lorenzo have been living together for a couple of days. Just the two of them in her *one-tomb apartment*. Who would've thought? Turns out, the space you really need is pretty relative. And Fiamma gets it now. It's kind of like freedom, made of whispered words, tiptoed steps, coffee sipped together in the morning, tiny bites, huge hopes, endless kisses, and breathless days.

Thanks to Roberto and his connections in Rome, Lorenzo got a job at a pizza place not far from Fiamma's apartment. He works from 7 p.m. until midnight, every single night, including weekends. It's technically part-time, but it's tough on him. Still, he's happy. He'd do anything to spend more time with Fiamma and earn some money too.

The job lets him pick her up after school, make her lunch, keep her company while she studies, quiz her on lessons she memorized, and eat an ultra-early dinner, more like afternoon tea or a hospital tray, before heading off with a breathless grin.

Those five hours he spends making pizzas always seem to crawl by, but they make coming home feel even sweeter. Fiamma usually waits for him on their fold-out couch, nose in a book, and the moment she hears the key in the lock, she runs to throw herself in his arms. Lorenzo always feels like he has to ask how the studying's going, pretending to quiz her on things he barely remembers. She usually brushes him off with a sigh and a tired, "Not now."

But the moments Lorenzo treasures most are the ones when he comes home to find her asleep, book draped across her face, arms stretched down at her sides. When he sees her like that, he could watch forever. He pauses at the half-open door, still holding his silly cow keychain, and just stares, until he finally leans in and wakes her with a kiss.

Papa,

Today's the anniversary of your death. Even after all these years, the memories still come crashing in, good and bad. Your strong arms turned to dry bones, unable to hug me. Your booming voice that I'll never hear again, not even to scold me. The salt in your hair that summer we spent by the sea. A whole storm of memories: the shells we collected on the beach, those pointless little pieces of calcium carbonate I sometimes want to cut myself with. And that spring sun…it stings, because it means I'll have to face another summer without you.

But this May feels different. I've finally decided to get help, to try and heal from my bulimia. I've also decided to be happy. To love myself. Not just let others love me. It won't be easy, but I think I can do it.

Eli and I finally talked. After her email, we met, opened up, cleared the air. We cried, and then laughed like we used to. And, as always, she was right: "Some people are just meant to stay in each other's lives once they've found each other." We're those people.

What happened between us only made our bond stronger.

Things with Lorenzo are going amazingly. I honestly couldn't ask for more. And as for Mom… lately, we've been talking more than ever. I've come to understand so much about her. And I think I'm finally ready to let her in, for real. No more pretending. No more lies.

Fiamma hasn't been to many plays in her life. And even fewer starring her own mother. Her mom's relationship with Giorgio marked the beginning of Fiamma's gut-level hatred for theater, and everything that came with it.

Maybe that's why Sara insisted so hard this time. That her daughter *had* to come. This tiny theater on the outskirts of Rome. Barebones set. Almost no audience.

Fiamma leaves early, no way she's going to be late. For once, she dresses simply: black jeans, a gray V-neck sweater, and a pair of modest block-heeled slingbacks. She chooses the outfit so no one will look at her. Tonight, her mother is the star, and she doesn't want to steal the spotlight. Wearing her understated clothes, she feels almost safe. But she can't explain why she's so on edge, like she's the one going on stage.

Looking around, Fiamma notices something: Giorgio isn't there. His name, his pompous last name, his stiff, arrogant presence, gone. Nowhere to be found in this little theater that might actually be smaller than her apartment.

A red curtain, a simple stage, six rows of blue plastic chairs, five seats each, and a storyline that's far from Pulitzer material:

A rich man planning to kill himself meets a mysterious and beautiful woman in a pub where he's having his 'last drink'. She's dressed simply, but she's stunning, magnetic, with a killer sense of humor. He's shocked to see she's reading Dostoevsky's White Nights, *his favorite story. They click. Sparks fly. He forgets his plan, invites her to his hotel room for a night of passion… where he's murdered by a hitman hired by a business rival. The woman? In on it the whole time.*

Sara plays the woman. She's more beautiful than ever on that bare little stage. Sitting in the front row, Fiamma catches every move. And she has to admit, her mother is *incredible.* The way she moves, her voice, her facial expressions, even her silences, they're pure theater. It's almost tragic to see such talent go unnoticed in front of a crowd this small.

There are maybe twenty people in the audience. Some younger, likely drama students pretending to be riveted; others older, probably parents or relatives of the cast. No one Fiamma recognizes. That stirs up a strange mix of feelings: awkwardness, because the only person she knows is her mom; pride, because her mom is killing it; and relief, because the play is going on, without Giorgio.

*

They agreed to meet up after the show at the little bar next door. Fiamma grabs a seat near the window, already resigned to a long wait, when she spots her mom rushing toward her, out of breath.

First thing she notices: no makeup, and her hair's a mess. Second: the outfit. Sara, who's always said gym clothes should *only* be worn at the gym or, at best, for a jog, is in a tracksuit and sneakers.

"Here I am! Didn't keep you waiting too long, did I?"

Sara collapses into the chair across from her daughter. It's like she's carrying the exhaustion of not just one show, but a whole lifetime of them, and tucked away somewhere in her sweatshirt, an endless string of future performances.

"I'm *beat*. Seriously. I don't think I've been this tired in… I can't even remember. I couldn't wait to get out of that makeup and costume. But mostly, I just couldn't wait to see you." Her voice softens, and she smiles.

Fiamma looks at her, really *looks*, and it's like she's seeing her mom for the first time. Yeah, she's tired. But there's something else, beneath the fatigue. A peace she hasn't seen in forever. A soft smile, framed by little laugh lines, hiding something unspoken. *Like she's let go of something. Or finally understood something she's been chasing for years. She looks… happy*, Fiamma thinks, feeling a swirl of curiosity, joy, and disbelief.

"You were amazing," is all she manages to say, even though what she really wants to blurt out is, *'I'm so proud of you, Mom. I mean it. I don't think I've ever been this proud.'*

"I finally said goodbye. I left Giorgio. I haven't seen him in days. I'm staying with a friend for now…"

Sara's words hit like fireworks. Not painful, but blinding. Fiamma freezes. She *hoped* this would happen, especially after their last talk and all those texts. But hearing the words out loud? That's something else. It makes a wild dream suddenly real.

"I couldn't wait to tell you in person…"

And then, silence. But not the heavy kind. It's light. Like a night sky. The kind of silence old friends fall into. A silence that leaves space for everything, not least, for the words that haven't yet been said.

Mom's sleeping over tonight. Well, I should say she's sleeping with us, because this is Lorenzo's home now too. I can't picture it without him.

It's going to be a mess at first. A total mess. Three adults in a shoebox apartment. But I couldn't let her stay at her friend's again. Not tonight. Not tomorrow. Maybe not the day after either. We'll figure it out.

I've decided to open the door to her. And I've decided to shut out everything that came with living in Giorgio's house, her blindness, her weakness, her failure to be a real mom. I'm leaving those years out in the hallway, like a dripping umbrella you don't want to bring inside.

It won't cost me anything to just forget. To love her. And maybe it'll do her good to be loved without having to face the ugly truth.

And now, seeing her here at two in the morning, standing there with her giant champagne-colored suitcase that takes up half the room, and that funny look on her face, that mix of worn-out and wide-eyed, like a forty-year-old girl, I just want to hug her. Hold her so tight and never let go. The way you hold on to the things you love and can't afford to lose.

We are so different, totally different souls, but somehow, we're the same. I get that now. Opposites that make each other whole. We're the spark that, once lit, can either become a wildfire or a tiny flicker that dies out.

But either way, that spark is enough to chase off the dark.

Outside, the sky looks like a chunk of coal, cut through by streaks of light. It hangs beyond the window like a tattered flag. Under that sky, in this tiny apartment we can barely afford, my mom, Lorenzo, and I are three crazy people, raising a toast with cheap beer in plastic cups.

We're celebrating like fools, loud and sincere. We're not worrying about the problems waiting for us tomorrow, because sometimes, it's enough to just celebrate. Even when there's no clear reason.

Tonight, we're celebrating a beginning. A promise.

The willingness to believe in each other. To let go of what was.

I don't know how long we'll last here, the three of us crammed into this matchbox. No clue how we'll make space without driving each other nuts. I don't even know if we'll have the money for rent or bills or groceries. But somehow, I believe we'll manage. Together, we'll make it.

Final exams are just a few days away, and school has felt like pure torture for Fiamma. She keeps thinking she'd be better off at home, focusing on the subjects that really trip her up. The tension in class is unbearable, it's like everyone else's anxiety has fused with hers, amplifying it, until it feels like a thick buzzing that presses down on her chest, making it hard to breathe. Sometimes she can't even tell one subject from another, and her thoughts spiral into the most random places. One moment she's sure the fractal theory her Math teacher is explaining belongs to Philosophy, and the next, the word *imperfect* morphs into *I'm perfect* and her mind drifts away.

Things aren't any better at home. She highlights so much in her textbook that the pages glow yellow like the sun, and all she wants to do is go outside and soak up the actual sunlight.

Her thoughts wander into strange corners, like imagining what she'd do if she were dropped into the labyrinth of Knossos without Ariadne's thread. Sometimes, she lets her imagination run wild on purpose. Because now, she knows that no matter what kind of maze life throws her into, she has Lorenzo, Elife, and her mom waiting for her on the other side. Fiamma knows she's never truly alone, no matter how things unfold. Maybe she'll never be completely lost. And that 'maybe', it holds power. It holds a quiet, incredible strength.

Because if it's true that happiness is fleeting and sly, ephemeral, older than we are, then maybe its clumsier sibling, unhappiness, is more patient, more forgiving. But even so, we're stronger than both. Stronger than any rigid expectation. Life might exist in just a single moment, in one sharp, beautiful now. And in this now, Fiamma can smell it. His scent. Her own. Theirs. It's a fragrance that clings to the air, grounding and intoxicating. The scent of what lingers, love that settles on skin, suspended in the air. The scent of kisses and embraces, of longing and exhaled hopes. It's the scent of "please stay," even as someone walks away. Because you're what remains, even when everything else fades.

A vivid scent, red lips brushing white wrists traced with anxious blue veins. She breathes it in like never before, and it gives her a kind of confidence she hasn't felt in a long time.

Today Mrs. Belardi, my teacher, took us back through Ovid's Metamorphoses, especially the story of the Phoenix. I think it must be her favorite, she's told it to us more than once. I have to admit, I love it too.

The Phoenix, that mystical bird, wasn't just legend, it was a symbol. It was said to be born in a fire beneath the sacred tree in Heliopolis, the Egyptian city of the sun. Every five hundred years, when it sensed its death coming, it would build a nest of scented branches and spices, sandalwood, myrtle, cedar, cinnamon, myrrh, and lie down to wait for the sun's fire. The flames would consume it, and from its ashes, a larva would rise, starting its life anew.

Mrs. Belardi got really passionate as she spoke, repeating how the Phoenix has been vital to art, literature, even religion. She reminded us how it symbolizes rebirth, the ability to rise again, again and again. Like the sun that disappears and returns every day. A cycle. Life, overcoming death.

I listened closely, especially when she drifted from the lesson. Honestly, it felt like she wasn't talking to us anymore, it was more of a monologue. Like she was telling herself to get back up. She said we have to learn to burn and not be afraid. To let go, but not forget who we were. That fire can change us, make us more beautiful. And maybe, just maybe, she was talking about her own heartbreak. Her husband leaving for another woman. Her lost youth. The wrinkles she no longer bothers to hide. The grief in her chest. But also the glimmer of starting over. Of becoming someone even stronger than before.

"How much longer?" Fiamma has to yell so Lorenzo can hear her over the wind, their helmets snug and the Red Fox speeding down the road.

"Almost there!" he shouts back, twisting the throttle.

They slice through the warm, sticky air, summer not quite here but close enough to taste, in the smell of sunscreen, ice cream, peach and coconut, cantaloupe and mint, blooming jasmine and hibiscus. It smells like the past. Like waking from a deep, happy sleep.

When she was little, summer meant Aunt Aida's licorice candies. Fiamma would visit her in August, in a tiny house tucked into the mountains. Aida was even tinier than the house, frail and hunched, always wearing a stained apron and carrying sweets in her pocket like they were contraband. She'd sneak one to Fiamma with a wink. First it was sweet, then bitter, staining her teeth black. She loved it. One candy turned into another, then another, until she was laughing at her darkened grin in the mirror.

Now Fiamma opens her eyes wide, soaking in everything around her. Then she shuts them again. And when she does, the entire world vanishes. The road, the lines, the cars, the sidewalks, the trees. Even the sky disappears. So does all the rest: the stress, the fear, the pressure of exams, her grudge against her mother, the hollow sadness on Elife's face. Gone. There's only one thing left: the sea. And a fluttering anticipation in her chest.

She clutches Lorenzo tighter. She wants to smell the sea before she sees it. That's what she decided when they first took off. She wants the memory of it to hit her first, salty and wild and alive. The smell that creeps into your brain and your bloodstream, claiming your whole body.

That scent is unique: grass, salt, seaweed, pebbles, cliffs, and fish. She wants it to jolt her awake. To snap her out of the numbness that's been weighing her down ever since the last time she saw the sea… with her dad. She doesn't even remember how old she was. Four? Five? Doesn't matter. What she remembers is the feeling, of joy and freedom. They were in Normandy, standing at the edge of the chalk cliffs of Étretat, tourists all around.

The cliffs looked like giant white teeth. And suddenly, her father had burst into song, the same silly tune he always sang in the shower:

Skippity-skip, sunshine's on its way,
oh what a sweet and magical day!

She remembered the burning shame of that moment. The embarrassment. Her mom's gentle smile. "Just ignore him," she'd said. But everyone was smiling, too, unsure whether to admire the view or him.

Now, flying along the coast with Lorenzo, she remembers that day. That exact second the sea announced itself. Because the sea always does, it makes itself known, loud and clear. And it doesn't care who you are. Rich or poor, first time or thousandth time. When it shows up, it's the same for everyone.

For some, it's the colors of the pebbles, for others it's jellyfish or mussels, or the polished shells scattered like confetti. But always, it's a gift. An offering. A hundred shades of blue.

Fiamma starts to count them in her head: aquamarine,

cerulean, robin's egg, sapphire, cobalt…

"We're here!" Lorenzo's voice yanks her out of the trance like an alarm clock after a sleepless night.

They're here. Standing at the edge of the ocean. Still in their helmets, dry feet on solid ground, yet already immersed. The breeze kisses their skin, the sun warm even though it's not officially summer. The sea's presence hits like a pat on the back. You made it.

And there's Fiamma, a young woman now, opening her eyes to see the child she used to be. She turns to Lorenzo and says, simply, "Thank you for taking me away."

Away from what?

Everything.

Away toward happiness. Toward the future. Or maybe back, toward something lost, when happiness was simple.

A wave crashes, like a woman collapsing into bed, leaving behind gifts: tiny shells, smooth stones, bits of glass. Fiamma picks up a seashell and holds it to her ear like she used to. Listens to the echo of the sea inside.

"Look how pretty… too bad it's chipped on one side."

"It doesn't matter. Stick it in your pocket, we're bringing it home anyway."

"Even if it's broken?"

"Especially if it's broken. Don't you remember Kintsugi? We'll find a way to fix it… and it'll be *beautiful*."

Here we are. Here she is. Here they are…

Fiamma closes her eyes again, holding the shell to her ear to catch the sea's whisper inside its fracture. Then she slips it deep into her pocket, like it's something rare, a treasure, a secret coin.

She opens her eyes and listens again, this time to the real sea just a few steps away, its voice louder now, closer, pulsing. She gazes at the cliffs, weathered by time, carved by wind, bold and jagged as they claw at the sky. Their sharp edges glow under the sun, their little shells drinking in the spray like thirsty mouths.

Here we are. Here it is. Here she is.

Fiamma and Lorenzo, hand in hand, walking along the shore. The sea follows them, beside them, around them, within them. It breathes in gentle waves and exhales quietly.

And now, they're no longer two.

There are three of them: Lorenzo, Fiamma, and the sea.

Today I realized I hadn't flipped the calendar in weeks. The days had passed, and I'd forgotten to notice them. I ripped the pages out and watched them burn in the sink. When the flames died, all that was left was a soft black pile of ash. I turned on the tap. The water washed it all away.

And I just stood there. Smiling.

Because today, I decided, I'm going to start living again. Even without you, Dad. Today, I'm taking back my life. My joy. My future.

Today, like the Phoenix, I'll rise from those ashes.

This novel is a work of fiction. Any resemblance to real people, events, or places is purely coincidental. The characters, situations, and settings are entirely the product of the author's imagination, and any similarity to actual persons, living or dead, is purely accidental.

A small request:

If you'd like to share your reading experience, leave a note, offer feedback or support, feel free to reach out through my website:

www.dananeri.com

If you enjoyed the book, I'd be incredibly grateful if you left a review on the platform where you purchased it. Your feedback means the world to me.
And if you'd like to send me a photo of you holding the book, I'd be delighted to receive it! With your permission, I'd love to share it on my social media channels as a way to celebrate this literary journey together.